HARVEY DUCKMAN PRESENTS...
VOL. 5

*A collection of sci-fi, fantasy,
steampunk and horror short stories*

6e

Published in paperback in 2020 by Sixth Element Publishing

Sixth Element Publishing
Arthur Robinson House
13-14 The Green
Billingham TS23 1EU
Tel: +44 1642 360253
www.6epublishing.net

© Sixth Element Publishing 2020

ISBN 978-1-912218-88-2

British Library Cataloguing in Publication Data. A catalogue record for this book is available from the British Library.

Printed in Great Britain.

CONTENTS

FOREWORD

BY BEN MCQUEENEY

Hello… ahead lies a series of short tales. They all have something to say, born from deep within the ether. Each one will converse with your soul, adhering your spirit with that of the authors. It is a truly a wonderous thing. I rejoice for you.

However, what do I have to say, among the next few lines? Something a little different perhaps? A game can be fun… sometimes. Can you find the answer in plain sight? Hidden between my words…

1. Hello again, weary reader. Welcome to Harvey Duckman Presents… Vol 5. But where are you from?

    a. The sky. →7

    b. Below the ground. →15

    c. The palace. →12

    d. A hovel. →14

2. Your soul is as dark as night. But what is more evil? →17

3. Wrong! The sounds you hear at night are not house sounds. →4

4. It is okay to be confused. Don't be afraid, reader. →1

5. You can remember what your mother looks like in your mind. Holding her picture inside your head. But what is looking at that picture? →1

6. I am sorry, it isn't you. →13

7. Must be cold. Do you have the power of all creation?
   a. Funny enough, yes. →11
   b. Erm… no? →4

8. A seed grows into a tree but what's its purpose? Is it to make more? Before returning to the cold dark earth from which it came.
   a. Agree. →16
   b. Disagree. →13

9. …

10. Perhaps… Can you remember what your mother looks like in your mind? Holding her picture inside your head? Have you got it? Great! But what is it that's looking at that picture? →6

11. Wow! Okay. But the answer you seek is more powerful than you. →13

12. Well, aren't you lucky. Please refrain from tripping over your suitcase of gold. What don't you have? →3

13. Have you worked it out?
    a. Yes. →9
    b. No. →1
    c. 3.1415926535 →4
    d. Global thermonuclear war.

14. Oh dear. But at least you have your health? Right?
    a. Yes… At least I think so. →10
    b. No… →8

15. Well, at least you have nice weather down there. But are you evil incarnate?
    a. Aha! You got me! →2
    b. What! No way. →4

16. History is just a collection of stories. The answer you seek knows all the stories in world. →1

17. This isn't the answer you're looking for. Evil doesn't deserve it. Your reflection in the mirror is always in the past. →13

•

Ben is a balding middle aged dad who published his first fantasy novel, The Spirit of Things, in 2020 after a creative awakening. When Ben's not running about after his three amazing kids and lovely Mrs, he tries to best men fifteen years younger at CrossFit for validation.

For more or to simply ask the answer to the foreword in this book, visit www.benmcqueeney.com

GERRY AND THE BERG

SCOTT HOWARD

1.

"Are you worried about global warming?" asked Gerry. The sun was approaching the horizon and the whole world seemed daubed in red. Behind him the Berg glowed pink.

"You do realise it's minus fifteen?"

"You know what I mean. Climate change."

"I don't think so," said the Berg. "I've been around a long time... but before I was me, I must have been snow and before that, water. If I melt, I'll just be water again."

"That's very philosophical of you."

"I can feel it happening sometimes."

Gerry looked at the enormous mass of ice looming over the boat. "What? Melting?"

"Maybe... You know water is just H_2O. Well, H_2O is a funny old molecule."

"You're in a funny old mood. What do you mean?"

"Maybe it's the sunset..."

Gerry snorted. "You were telling me about H_2O."

"Well, there's an oxygen atom, and two hydrogens, and they stick together because the hydrogens each share an electron with the oxygen – a covalent bond. They stick on like the ears on a Mickey Mouse hat. But the ears are a bit askew, and so the electrical charges are also a bit askew, so one end of the molecule is electrically positive and the other is negative. This means that each water molecule is attracted to those around it and they bond together with what are called hydrogen bonds. They're not separate, but stick together in a giant cluster, a gel."

"I think I've read this somewhere. More like one big molecule?"

"Sort of, but the bonds break and reform very quickly – under 200 femtoseconds. Anyway, all this means water has some odd properties – a very high boiling point for its weight, high surface tension... it's why I float!"

The colour had drained from the sea and from the sky while the Berg talked. A cold wind made the suddenly slate sea break into chop. The hollow sound echoed up from where it slapped against the hull.

"That's what I feel sometimes," said the Berg. "The hydrogen bonds inside me are locked down, but on my surface, where I touch the water and the air, they're fizzing away, spreading me out... 'oceanic boundlessness' as Freud might've said."

Gerry regarded the Berg with sadness. "I'm sorry we're melting you. We're horrible sometimes."

The Berg groaned and cracked like a gunshot. The water all around shivered.

"Ha! That's very polite of you. I'll last a bit longer yet though. My hydrogen bonds are very stable. It takes the same amount of energy to warm me from -160°C up to 0°C as it does to melt me."

"Really? Wow."

"Indeed."

A silence fell between them. The sun was long gone. Hard, brilliant stars were appearing overhead. Gerry couldn't feel his toes anymore.

"You know," said the Berg eventually, "you're looking much healthier than you have been."

"I've been eating O'Neill."

"Oh."

"When the lifeboat capsized, his was the only body I could fish out. He's been frozen down in the hold ever since."

"Hmmm. What does he taste like?"

"I've got nothing to cook him with. Frozen, hairy, greasy, horrific pork? I don't know. I can taste him in my mouth all the time but I'm trying not to think about it."

"Sorry. I suppose it's a bit like me and the water."

"Just shut up, okay?"

2.

"Are you *drunk*?"

"No."

"You swore to me there was no more booze down there!"

"I'm not fucking drunk!" shouted Gerry miserably.

"I had grease on my glasses, and I started running them under hot water and one of the lenses cracked because it's minus fucking thirty. I can't see shit."

"Oh. Sorry." The Berg glinted in the sunshine. "I thought you ate all the grease. And hot water?"

"Not edible grease. Grease grease. For the engine."

"Hmmm." The Berg drifted away from the boat a little as if to get a better look at Gerry; wavelets sploshed energetically against the hull. "Your head doesn't look oversized."

"My head's not oversized! What's that got to do with it? You're really being very irritating today."

"Sorry. Something's too big though, more likely your eye than your actual head. That's why you can't see. Your eye focuses light on a point in front of your retina. If your eye was smaller, you wouldn't have a problem."

Gerry kicked a bulkhead. "Well I do have a problem! I'm starving to death and freezing to death. I spend my days talking to a fucking iceberg. And now I can't see!"

The Berg trickled sulkily. "Well, if that's the way you feel… we don't have to talk. I suppose it means nothing that I could help you get a new prescription."

"A new prescription?"

"That's the spirit!" said the Berg, butting against the boat and sending a clatter of shards onto the deck. "Have you got a ruler?"

"Uhh… I'll see if I can find one."

Gerry returned twenty minutes later to find the sun had gone in and the Berg floating in a stew of sea ice that had seemingly appeared from nowhere. The temperature had dropped alarmingly.

"Got it? Great. Now measure the distance between your eyeball and the lens you have left in your glasses. Actually don't! It's pretty nippy out here. Don't want the ruler stuck to your eyeball. It's probably a centimetre. We'll say a centimetre."

"Okay. Where did you learn all this anyway?"

"I'm made out of ice. I'm reflecting, refracting, all that stuff. Optometry's easy. Now. Which lens is broken? Left? So, hold the ruler up to your cheek and close your right eye. Look along the ruler and move your finger towards you till you can focus on it. How far away's that?"

"About ten inches."

"Metric, man! We're not barbarians."

"Sorry. Maybe 25cm."

"Wow, you are blind. Okay. 25cm is your far point. That's the point your left eye focuses at when it's resting. If you weren't myopic that'd be infinity."

"Infinity?"

"Technically, yes. The moon, the stars, they'd be in focus."

"Oh."

"Okay. So, you need a diverging lens, one that's concave on both sides. That's more bad news actually."

"More?"

"If you ever need to start a fire in the wilderness you have the wrong type of lens. It won't focus the sun's rays to a point."

"That's okay. When I get too weak to move, I've still got a few matches and a cup of diesel put aside. I'm going to set the boat on fire and be warm again before I die."

The Berg groaned and cracked. A tern that had been perched out of sight on its far side flew off across the water with a mournful cry.

"That's the spirit! Getting your sense of humour back – that's good, just let me know before you torch the thing so I can drift off a bit."

Gerry smiled. He didn't want to admit it, but the Berg's high spirits were making him forget the sense of hopelessness that had descended on him ever since the lens had cracked in his numb fingers.

"So, your diverging lens will make things appear to be at your far point. It'll move things all the way from infinity to 25cm from your face. Neat, hey? We just need to figure out the focal length for your lenses. That's just your far point in metres, so 0.25, minus the distance of your lens from your eye, call it one, so let's say 0.24. You bang a negative in front of that and there's your focal length! Negative 0.24."

"I thought prescriptions were in whatsits… dioptres."

"No problem at all. Dioptres are just a made-up measurement that optometrists like to use. They're just one divided by the focal length. So… one divided by -0.24 equals… -4.16."

"Nice mental arithmetic."

"Thank you. Now optometrists like the steps to be in

0.25 increments, so your prescription, Gerry, for your broken lens, is… -4.25!"

"Wait, I thought you were getting me new glasses?"

"Pay attention. I said *prescription*. Where am I going to get new glasses? I'm an iceberg. The South Pole is just there over the horizon."

3.

Gerry leaned against the binnacle and bit into the nectarine. Juice dribbled down his chin and he sucked frantically at the flesh of the fruit to avoid losing any more.

"Where on Earth did you find that?" asked the Berg.

"Below decks," said Gerry, slurping greedily. "There's a whole box of them."

"But you've been eating nothing but pemmican for nearly two months now."

"I must have missed them. Nooks and crannies down there. Yesterday I found a book of crosswords."

The Berg cracked alarmingly. It was a sunny day and light blared back from its surface and hurt Gerry's eyes.

"Nevertheless."

Gerry shrugged and continued savouring the nectarine.

"They're radioactive, you know."

Gerry spat the stone noisily overboard. "Bullshit."

"Well, not strictly radioactive, but bred with the aid of radiation."

Gerry, who had been about to go down to get another one, turned back. "Really?"

"Really. After World War Two everyone was trying to find peaceful uses for atomic energy. Just using it to vaporise Japanese people was giving it a bad name. They made atomic gardens to try and harness its mutagenic properties."

"Wasn't this a *Simpsons* episode?"

The Berg trickled furiously. The sunshine had made its whole surface run with meltwater.

"Don't be facetious. It's entirely true. They set up circular fields with a radioactive slug, cobalt-60 or something equally nasty, tied to a pole in the middle. The idea was you planted a wedge of a particular crop and let the radiation work its mutation magic. Close to the centre everything just died. Farther back though you'd get weird effects like giant fruit or strangely coloured leaves and flowers."

"Cool."

"Actually, I'm finding it distinctly warm," said the Berg.

"You're very grumpy today. So, what happened with the mutant plants? And how did they harvest this stuff?"

"The pole with the radiation source could be retracted into the ground, then workers would come in to examine what had happened to the plants."

"Voila, radioactive nectarines."

"Actually, peach trees mutated by radiation whose progeny are what, today, we know as the nectarine."

"I'll be damned. Any other successes?"

"Mint oil."

"Mint oil?"

"Mint is particularly susceptible to fungal wilt. The

Americans irradiated hundreds of thousands of shoots and then planted them in wilt-infested fields. The resulting wilt-resistant cultivar, Todd's Mitcham as I believe it's called, is now the standard crop used in the world's mint oil industry. You brushed your teeth with some this morning."

"I ate the last of the toothpaste six weeks ago."

"You're going to wish you hadn't when it comes time to get all those bits of nectarine out of your teeth."

"Very funny. So, nectarines, mint oil… they give it up after that?"

"Oh, it's still happening. Not as popular as back in the '60s and '70s but they still use it to try and breed new plant varieties today. The last success we know of was the 'Rio Star' – a particularly red variety of grapefruit."

"That we know of?"

"It's all very hush hush. Genetic engineering. Radioactive mutants. You know – things you don't want associated with your product."

"So how do you know about it?" asked Gerry, turning to head below deck again. The sun had moved, and he was in the Berg's shadow. When he tried to lick some of the nectarine juice from his beard it was already starting to freeze.

"A hippy who was down here in 1976 told me. They parked their boat alongside me for a few days. He used to like to come and talk to me."

"Talk to you? You're an iceberg."

"He was taking a lot of acid."

4.

"God, I'm so bloody cold! I really don't know how you can stand it!" screamed Gerry, breath exploding into a small cloud that froze and tinkled onto the deck. "Look! That can't be good."

"No, not good at all," said the Berg.

"All this energy locked up around me too. If I had some magic power... If I could just split one measly atom, I'd be warm as toast."

"No, I did the numbers on that," said the Berg dejectedly. "The phrase 'splitting the atom' is all very exciting, but really, you're just getting a lot of atoms to move from one state to another – transmuting them – in fusion from hydrogen to helium, and liberating the difference."

"Not with my magic power. I'd split it. $E=MC^2$. Total mass to bloody energy!"

The Berg shifted uncomfortably.

"Even then it doesn't work. Take hydrogen. The mass of one mole of hydrogen is 1.008g. In that mole there are 6.02×10^{23} molecules of hydrogen."

"That's a lot."

"Indeed. So, divide one by the other and you can see that the mass of a single hydrogen molecule is 1.67×10^{-24}g."

"That's not much."

"It's 0.00000000000000000000000167 grams."

"Especially when you put it like that."

"And that's molecular hydrogen, so two actual atoms. If we're talking about a single atom, it weighs half that again. Plug that into $E=MC^2$ and your magical power gives you 0.0000000752 joules when it splits the single hydrogen atom you've plucked out of the air."

"Shit."

"If we convert it to calories, to warm one cubic centimetre of water by one degree Celsius, you'd need to split around 56 million hydrogen atoms."

"Hand me the axe."

The Berg laughed its deep laugh. Gerry felt it in his bones. The water around the boat vibrated.

"How did you get so good at maths, anyway?"

"Wolfram Alpha – that thing's amazing."

"Wait, you've got internet?"

5.

Gerry threw the orange into the water and slapped his hand against the gunwale in frustration.

"They can't have thought that! That's what we think now. They didn't have the bloody scientific apparatus to magnify something that much."

The Berg shifted slightly, voice amused. "So if you went and asked some random idiot what the surface of an orange would look like if you were one hundredth of a millimetre tall, what would they say? They don't have the scientific apparatus either."

"As a culture they do. They may not have ever used a scanning electron microscope, but they've seen enough trippy animation at the start of movies to know that things aren't just… I don't know, *smooth*."

"Who says the ancient Greeks, or any primitive culture, saw the very small as smooth?"

"Well they can't have seen it as bloody molecular, or atomic!"

"The Greeks saw it as atomic."

"That was just a theory, an extension of Plato's perfect forms. If they cut the skin of an orange smaller and smaller, they wouldn't get structure, cells walls, amino acids – they'd get tiny orange spheres. Ancient Greek atoms."

"But that's what we get now. It's just a difference in how we get there."

"Tiny orange spheres?"

"When you use your imagination to zoom in on this orange, down through cells walls and such, what do your atoms look like?"

"Okay, coloured spheres."

"Not electron clouds surrounding subatomic particles that are best described as probability densities?"

"Okay! Okay!" Gerry turned away and looked out across the grey ocean. There was a slight chop and the wind had turned even colder. The Berg loomed behind him, waves slapping against its base with a fractured, hollow sound.

"All I'm bloody saying," he said, turning back to the wall of ice, "is that it would be interesting to know how ancient cultures imagined the very small, given that, although some of them may have possessed the philosophical idea of the atom, the vast majority did not. None of them had a microscope, and so would have been totally unaware of the minute complexity of everyday objects."

The Berg rumbled in appreciation. "Well put. Yes, that's an interesting thought. Personally, I have no idea how they imagined such things. Nobody really got down here much except in the last one hundred years or so, and they were all too busy killing whales and freezing to death to stop and chat."

6.

"Look what I found!" shouted Gerry triumphantly, waving what appeared to be a sausage in the Berg's direction.

"A sausage?"

"A sausage!"

"You didn't make it out of O'Neill, did you?"

Gerry looked around wildly. Sea ice had closed in over the past week and the boat was sitting in a jagged plain. The wind had abated overnight, and the resulting silence was terrifying. The Berg stood nearby.

"I'd forgotten about O'Neill."

The Berg trickled sadly.

"I found it in Kopotkin's pillow, in the pillowcase. I think he'd been saving it."

"Didn't you tell me Kopotkin was a filthy animal? Of all your crewmates, you said he was the only one whose death, what was the phrase you used, whose 'death was a blessing'."

"He was."

"And now you're going to eat his sausage."

Gerry involuntarily started drooling at the thought.

"Be careful you don't get sick."

"I ate O'Neill, didn't I?"

"Sausages are far worse. You might get botulism. First you feel tired, then there's muscle weakness, soon you're paralysed. Out here on the deck you won't last five minutes if you're not moving around."

Gerry, who had been walking back and forth to keep warm while sniffing the sausage, looked up at the mass of ice above him. "Do you think that's likely?"

"Probably not. It's probably too cold."

"Why sausages anyway? I thought botulism was the one you got from tinned food."

"They first isolated the bacteria in preserved meats. 'Botulus' is Latin for 'sausage'. You know, if your sausage does have some growing in it, you could sell it."

"What?"

"You get botulism because the bacteria produce botulinum toxin – same stuff they use for Botox. It's the most expensive naturally occurring substance on Earth. Also, the most poisonous."

Gerry eyed the sausage. "What about plutonium?"

The Berg shivered, dropping shards of ice on the frozen plain with a sound like smashing crockery. "Positively healthy in comparison – botulinum is 320,000 times more poisonous than plutonium. You could kill over a million people with a gram of the stuff."

"Probably not much in my sausage though."

"Hmmm yes, probably only enough to kill you."

"Why are we injecting it in our foreheads then?"

"I really couldn't say. Vanity?"

"Very funny."

"Thank you. No, someone from the UN who was down here explained it to me once. There were fears the Nazis might have been developing it as a chemical warfare agent in World War Two. After the war, the Americans took over the research. A bloke who'd been refining it for the US Army teamed up with an ophthalmologist and eventually they created Botox. It was originally used to treat people with a twitchy eyelid. The other uses came later. Preventing muscles from contracting can be very useful."

"Wait, why did the UN guys know all this?"

"Iraq had been following the Nazis' and the Americans' lead. He'd been a weapons inspector."

"Wow! I thought all that WMD stuff was fake though. Unknown unknowns and all that."

"You're thinking 2003. This was back in 1991. The Gulf War."

"You really keep up with the news, don't you?"

"To be honest, there's very little else to do. People like yourself turning up and chatting to me are a rarity."

"People trapped on their broken boat. Slowly starving to death."

"Exactly."

Scott Howard is a Melbourne-based public servant, Excel nerd, and writer of scifi, weirdness and occasional poetry. God has tried to kill him twice, so far.

Find out more at http://idiomzero.blogspot.com

THE SKY'S THE LIMIT

KATHRINE MACHON

The Rainhill Trials, October 1829

Robert rubbed his face, adding another smear of grease to his forehead. "Why, oh why did I agree to this?" His sleeves were rolled up, neck cloth unwinding as he made his final checks.

"You can't be getting pigeon-livered now," I said, though in truth my nerves jangled like keys on a housekeeper's ring. "You know the world needs to change. Before it's too late."

"I did it for the challenge, not for your cause," Robert replied with a hint of acid. "I knew I could build something better than anyone else. Something that would win this race."

"The lure of the five hundred pounds prize money had nothing to do with it, I suppose."

Robert huffed in reply and I went to stand next to him. We stared up at the metal monster squatting in the centre of the shed. Its smokestack disappeared into the night's shadows while the great curve of its boiler gleamed dully in the lantern light.

My nerves dissolved in a spark of euphoria and I caught Robert's shoulder. "You really did it."

His teeth showed in a brief smile. "You wouldn't believe the excuses I had to make to have all those extra rivets added to the firebox."

The euphoria wavered. "It will be strong enough for their heat?" I'd seen the results of exploding metal.

"Of course," he reassured, but his lips narrowed in a tight line. "Are you sure about this, Tom? They're banned for good reason."

"Good reason!" I stepped away from him. "They're not dangerous, just hungry because we steal their coal. And for that we're driving them to the edge of extinction."

He sighed. "Don't start your spiel on me. I don't want to hear it." A shiver ran through him from more than the chill October air. "Lord knows what my father will make of this."

"Don't worry," a voice said from the doorway and we both jumped. "We'll probably be deported before you have to face the great George Stephenson."

"Ben," I breathed. "At last. I was starting to worry." I glanced past him. "Where are the others?"

"Not far behind." He gave a heavy cough, spat, then touched his cap in brief apology to Robert. "The air's thicker than in a whore's armpit out there." He moved further into the shed then gave a little gasp. "So this is it?"

"The Rocket," Robert said, patting the steam engine like it was a favourite horse.

Ben crept closer, eyes wide, mouth open. "A rare beast you've built there."

I hid a smile. Trust Ben to consider the engine the beast in the room. His forehead gleamed with sweat and after a moment he pulled out a handkerchief and scrubbed his brow. It came away sooty, like everything else in this country since the huge industrial factories had been built.

My own forehead was equally beaded with moisture. "Better than a hot water bottle," I said, patting the bulge hidden beneath my shirt.

Ben chuckled as a matching bump squirmed under his jacket. "And getting restless."

Robert backed away from us both. "What type are they, exactly?"

"Don't worry. Just rock dragons. Small and easy to tame."

"It will need more than two to heat this," Robert said, rubbing his palms against his trousers.

"There are more on the way."

Robert groaned and retreated to a bench at the side of the shed. There was the clink of metal and a flash of reflected lantern light as he raised a flask to his mouth and swigged. Dutch courage. I could have done with some of that myself, but one of us needed a clear head.

The bulge under my shirt fidgeted, claws grazing my skin. I loosened the ties at my neck, letting the little black dragon, about the size of a teapot, wriggle free. It climbed onto my shoulder, tilted its long head and watched me with bright eyes. I scratched its jaw, the scales rasping against my finger, and it purred.

"Time to get you settled," I said.

The door of the firebox squealed as I opened it. There was enough room for five or six rock dragons to fit comfortably. Or just one of the larger species. But if we were going to break the law, we should probably start small and hope it was overlooked. That would only happen if we won this race.

The dragon fluttered from my shoulder and into the firebox. Ben's followed, and they circled the space, sniffing and cooing, dark scales glinting. Dragons had a thing about iron.

"We're pioneers of a better world." Ben had a soppy smile on his face as he watched them.

His words swelled warm in my chest, burning stronger than any courage that spirits might have raised. Today, Robert and I would risk everything for a dream. A dream which was about more than the dragons.

"It's almost dawn." Ben's words jolted me back. "The others should be here by now. Come on. Let's check for them."

Leaving Robert snoring quietly on his bench, we went outside into the dark. Frosted grass crunched under boots and I paused, straining to hear. Where were they? But the factory smoke that hung heavy in the air muffled sound as well as hiding the bright wink of the stars.

"There," Ben said softly as shapes detached themselves from the night and trotted towards us.

"Sorry," someone whispered. "We almost ran into the watchman."

"Let's get them inside." Ben waved the group towards the shed, leaving me staring into the fading night. Not long now. My stomach tightened at the thought. This had to work. We had to prove the old stories were true. Dragons could be our friends, warming our homes and lighting our lanterns. It was only greed that had turned us into enemies – this battle for the dark rocks under the ground to fuel our growing machines.

We had to change things for them and for us. The race was our chance.

"Engines are weighed in at eight," Ben said from behind me and I twitched.

The darkness was slipping away now, the horizon threaded with grey which merged into the dull smudge that was Liverpool. Industrial chimneys cut the skyline, already pouring smoke upwards. The only brightness was a sudden glint of light on water as the rising sun silvered the slick surface of the Mersey.

I nodded. "Almost time."

•

The Rocket had been weighed and run by hand up to the starting post. Water and coal were loaded and carriages attached.

Robert straightened his frock coat and pressed his beaver hat more firmly onto his head. "If I'm going to be detained by the constable, I'm going to look good for it."

He stood tall on the engine's footplate. Before it, the track stretched for a mile and a half, two straight lines disappearing into a pinprick in the distance. A crowd had gathered beyond rope barriers which stopped them approaching the engines. Ten or fifteen thousand souls, perhaps. Gentlemen in the latest fashion wore elaborate waistcoats and neck ties. Women in their bell-shaped skirts clutched children's hands. The air was busy with the murmur and shout of the crowd and the oily scent of hot pies. A snatch of music from the band, trumpets and trombones, reached us on a stray gust of breeze. My insides clenched like a sheet in a clothes mangle. So many witnesses. Soon there'd be no hiding what we'd done.

The judge was eyeing the pile of coal in our tender. Not much compared to what the other engines had used, but he couldn't ask why we carried so little – all designs were secret.

As the man circled to the front of the engine, Robert nudged me. "Go on then."

I dug my shovel into the coal heap and opened the firebox. The dragons were curled up together in a jumble of scaly limbs and wings. They stirred at the scent of the coal. Bright eyes opened and they scrambled to their feet, bobbing in excitement and making tiny peeping noises as I let the coal trickle in. They fell on it, squabbling for the best pieces like a mischief of magpies, gulping down whole chunks. I added another shovelful before gently closing the door.

"Is that all they need?" Robert questioned.

I nodded. "Best not to over-vex them. Let them build heat slowly."

We waited in silence. Robert was pale-faced and I supposed I was too. On a side-track, evidence of engines that had run before us and failed was all too clear: the broken boards of the Cycloped where the horse had fallen through the drive belt to burst from the floor of the engine; the engineers working on the cracked cylinder of the San Pareil engine. And now it was our turn. The Rocket. I reached out a hand to the firebox, then snatched it back. Hot so soon?

A thin trickle of steam escaped the safety valve and Robert adjusted the levers. "It's bubbling already." He checked the pressure gauge. "Lord in Heaven…" He took a deep breath. "The rivets had better withstand this swift climb in temperature."

"I believe in your design," I said, but my voice quivered.

Robert gave a grim smile. "And I'm putting my faith in your dragons. Let us hope we don't both regret it."

The judge appeared from the front of the engine. "Indicate when the steam pressure has reached fifty pounds per square inch," he instructed.

Robert leaned over the gauge and swallowed. "Already there."

The judge's eyebrows shot up, wriggling like a pair of startled caterpillars. "Indeed." His pencil dashed across his notebook. "Well then." He pointed to a man waiting at the side of the track who raised a large flag.

Robert adjusted the control levers one last time, took a slow breath and nodded to the man. The flag dropped. We both hauled on the break handle and the pistons juddered, inched downwards and the wheels turned. The train eased forward in a clank of metal, jolted to stillness for a second as the couplings joining the thirteen-ton load tightened, then continued its forward roll.

The smokestack chimney was devoid of the billowing black clouds that had streamed from the other engines to engulf the crowds. How long before someone noticed?

Robert and I shared a glance.

"No turning back," he said.

Each downward thrust of the pistons came faster in a rush and hiss of sound, vibrating the engine and rattling our teeth. We gripped the safety rail, white knuckled and sweating despite the chill autumn air.

Racing children, waving handkerchiefs, tried to keep pace with the engine, but our growing speed quickly left them panting in our wake. The crowd's faces blurred past us, their shouts swallowed up in the clickety-clack of the wheels on the track.

Wind tore at my neck cloth, tugging the ends free to fly behind me like flags, threatening to rip it loose completely. I scrubbed tears from my cheeks and gasped air into lungs that didn't want to inflate. Surely man was never designed to go this fast? And still our speed increased. Beside me,

Robert was shouting and waving his arms but the wind tossed his words to the heavens.

The one-mile marker grew from a speck to a looming reality. No one had run the course this fast. As we thundered by the mark, Robert threw open the safety valves. Steam and dragons' breath rushed into the air. That scent. A mix of hot metal and gunpowder. Unmistakable. Now everyone would know.

The rattle of the engine and rush of the wind had stoppered my ears. As the train slowed, rumbling towards a halt, the crowd became clear. Gaping mouths, pointing fingers.

Robert leapt from the footplate and danced a wobbly-legged jig. All smiles. Then sound snapped back into focus. The crowd didn't care. They were cheering.

Newspaper men ducked under the rope barrier to call questions at Robert. An artist was sketching a picture of The Rocket with me still on the footplate. From my high position, the words he wrote underneath were clear.

"Stephenson's Rocket wins race in grand, smoke-free finale."

A smile stretched my face. We'd done it. Really done it. The man understood and tomorrow the newspapers would share with the nation our vision of a better future.

Not just safety for the dragons, but clean skies for us.

Kathrine Machon is a lover of all things magical. She lives on the island of Jersey and spends her spare time scribbling stories about fantastical characters and places. She has had a number of short stories published and hopes one day to have her name on the front cover of a novel.

THE SALMON SWIM BOTH WAYS

MARK HAYES

It calls to me.

It calls to the salt in my veins.

It calls across the aeons, as it has always called my kind.

It calls me back to the waves, back to the ocean, back to the depths.

It calls to me…

I knew I was different, I always knew. I knew from the first days of my memories, I knew and I understood. I was not like other children. I was awkward, shy. But it was more than awkwardness, more just than shyness. I was not like them, I would never be like them. I knew, just as my mother knew.

She never said, but she knew.

It was the blood in my veins that set me apart from the world. Blood that was part my mothers, but in no part the blood of the man I called father, though he knew I am sure, as I always did, I could not be his son. I knew that in my blood, and in the salt that lay within it.

He loved me, the man I called father. Loved his strange

son, the strange child, so sullen, so haunted. He loved me as a father should, though I could not love him back. For all I knew him all my days he remained a stranger to that which dwelt within me, to that which my heart pumped, to that which coursed through arteries, to that inner self that spoke to me, the very blood in my veins.

I loved him not though he did me no wrong in life, that man I called father. He raised me as he thought best, despite knowing, I am sure, that I was the cuckoo's get. He raised me as his own, as if my blood was his, called me son and set me on the path he felt true. So though I never loved him in return, it's true, he had my respect all the same. Perhaps that is better, to have respect, even when love cannot flourish. What bitterness may lie within my breast, lay there not for him, and parted as we have now been by death's great veil some ten years, I respect him still, and mourn him in my own way, that man I called father.

But it is better we are parted now, I know this too is true. For I feel the call. Feel it and fear it. And fear most that should I deny it I shall never know the peace in life he who was not my father sought to instil with a father's devotion and kindness born in the wisdom of years.

As for my mother, she has crossed that final veil too, though her passing is less than a year past.

Her passing was I believe a blessing for her, but it felt a curse for me, for ever close was the bond between us. Mother and son. She tied me to the world I knew, to the ground upon which I walked the places that were of her.

For the blood that called me to the salt shared my veins still with that from her.

But her passing was a blessing still, for she waned in the years since he I called father passed. My mother lost the zest for life which he had given her in such abound. Then, as he became a memory, sickness took hold of her. Ate away at her from within, till she was less than the shell of whom she had once been. But even then, with the spark of life near gone from her eyes she told me nothing of the truth of me. She never told me of my getting. Not in life. I think at times she chose this path not to sully my memory of he who was not my father. Perhaps she thought I did not know what lay within my blood. Perhaps she thought I did not hear that call within my veins. The call of salt to salt, of blood to water, the call of that which I was in truth. But I knew, I always knew and I always felt the call, no matter how clouded it was by the pills of the men in white coats. It waxed and waned like the moon grip upon the sea, but the call was always there.

When I was young, not yet a man, only thirteen summers gone, I felt that call all the stronger. Stronger than ever before. It called to me, to my blood, to that which dwelt within. Called to me and drew me to it, a call I could resist no more. One August day, with the sun burning down, I found myself upon a road I had never known before. With money stolen from the kitchen drawer, I went south, ever south towards the call, first by foot, then bus, then train, then bus and finally by foot again. Until I found myself on a crafted plain. A place of wood and iron, built for a prince once regent long ago in the bright town to the south of my London home, and there I walked with purpose unknown, answering that which drew me on, that voice that echoed deep within, that endless mournful call, of surf and wave and the deep below. A call to return beneath waves of surf, where the sun cannot go. Home to the darkness of the depths.

I walked that pier's length in a daze, knowing not the passing hour of the day, until I reached the railings at the end and looked out across the rolling waves. And all the while it called to me, the salt in my blood, the salt of the sea. *'Come home, return, be what you are, be still, beneath, in the depths below, join us, child of salt and water, join us no, child, come home.'*

I stood there, I know not how long, as the sun did move throughout the sky and shadows lengthened on salt crusted boards. I watched the sea I had never seen before. Mother, in wisdom born at the breast, had seen never to take me to that ever-changing border, the divide between land and wave. So she would not risk the shore with a child born of salt, not till I was fully formed, least the call take me beyond that border, but in that wrong she was I'm sure, for as a child the call was weak, a nagging feeling undefined, a tug at the sleeve, not a pull full formed. But as I grew from child to man, only stronger would that call become, and not the call of waves themselves but of that which lay beyond them and beneath. The call of the darkness, the depths, the abyss. The call of the plenty where the land is barren. And each year told, the call grew stronger, and lessen did the urge to resist.

And so I stood there at that rail, as night fell and sun sank below the horizon line as I would sink beneath the waves. Then in the moon's full glow, I mounted the rails, for the call is always stronger with the moon above. That silvery mistress of the sun who creates the tides within the sea, and the tides within my blood. I climbed the rails, the first, then second. As I climbed, the call came stronger still.

Join us, return home, child of our salt, join us…'

On the third rail I stood, balanced there, looking down on the crashing waves below. Dizzy with the smell of brine, the sound of the ocean and that inner call, the pull within my blood. I stepped forward, knowing it would mean my fall. Fear gripping me, but tinged with exultation I had never felt before, I stepped forward into the nothing, and…

The man who grabbed my arm was strong. He pulled me back, over the rails and back to the platform of wood and iron. I fought him, with fight borne of panic, of that calling urge within my blood, that desperate need that swelled within me. But he held me tight till the coppers came, and they walked me back across the wood to the land I would have left forever, the call within fading with each step. And as it faded I found a new emotion within me, a fear which had no name, not a fear of the sea, or of that voice within, but a fear of myself, of the blood that coursed through my veins, of everything that I was.

Fear of myself, and fear of the call that drew me to the crashing waves. A fear of the sea, and the longing for it, that clutched so tightly at my soul.

They took me home when the sun returned. Home to where my mother wept. Home to where the man who wasn't my father waited with words of kindness and understanding, words that did not understand nor were ever truly kind.

"It's a teenage thing," the copper said who brought me back to them, "a lot of lads go through it, silly urges, a cry for help, nothing more, take him to a counsellor, let them talk to him, I'm sure he'll be fine, probably scared himself half to death, and that's no bad thing at that…"

Words, there were so many words. Words that pretended to understand but knew nothing about what they spoke. Yet he who was not my true father took them all in, and my mother too. She grasped at them, held them tight and did not let the truth come out. The truth she knew, but never told.

I knew the thoughts that passed through her mind. *Better this be simple, better he be normal, just the teenage thing, nothing more, no call of blood, of sea and surf, just teenage angst, those normal things, same as any other mother's child…'*

This I knew she wanted to believe and in truth I did so too. Better that, than the true, better that than the call within my blood, and for a while I came to believe it so, though I knew deep within my soul those words were false, no normal for me, a child of the sea.

They gave me pills, the men in white coats and Arran

sweaters. Pills to keep me calm, to dull my mind and hold me in check. And the call, well, it faded for a while, became a forgotten thing, but yet deep within, still there, still ripe with hunger, ripe with need. Then he who was not my father died, and with his death the call returned.

They found me washed up on a shore I did not know, naked, cold and lost of soul. I remembered not how I came to be there, nor remembered why the sea rejected me then. Did it reject my half salt blood, or was it that I was not ready then, still not fully formed a man. In time I would believe the latter, even know it as a truth. But at first when they found me I was distraught. A rejection felt as never before. It hurt me deep within, hurt me more than the pain of the passing of he I had called father did not. A rejection as profound as it could be, the rejection of my blood, of my salt, by the sea.

More pills followed, more doctors, and the endless worry of my mother. Without the man who was her husband to calm her worries, the rock around which she built her life, to tell her it would all be fine, she worried. Worried herself into an illness, an illness from which she would never recover. For that, for the longest time I blamed myself. Myself and the men in white coats, and those endless pills that numbed my soul.

When I should have been caring for her, she cared for me more than herself. A mother's love. A mother's worry. While the pull of the salt grew stronger each passing month, as the tides are pulled by the moon. Raising and falling, waxing and waning but always there always growing stronger still. She tried to keep her secrets, to never tell the truth of it. But in the end as her illness took her away from me, her mind went back to the beginning and the truth behind my blood and the call within it.

She was young when she met him. A true son of the sea, drawn as they are to the emptiness that is the land when the time comes to mate. A calling as strong as that which haunted my blood. His time with her was fleeting. A few weeks, and when he left once more, returning to the tide and the deep, she was ashen. But within her grew his seed, his salt, and that which would become me.

She passed, and with her passing had passed all hold the land had upon my id. The call grew stronger, drawing me back to the division, to the places of sand and surf.

The pills from the men in white coats were forgotten, a bottle of numbness left in a bathroom behind me. And as the numbness left me, the call in my blood grew ever stronger. Till it brought me at last to that village by the sea, the place where my mother had met him first. The place of tides and salt. Of screeching seabirds and brine. And there I waited, while the moon came full once more, while the tide rose its highest and the call was at its strongest.

And then...

•

"Third one this year," the constable said, placing the abandoned clothing into a plastic evidence bag.

"Aye," his sergeant said, scrawling in his notebook the details found in the wallet that had been likewise abandoned on the shore.

"Why do they do it?" pondered the constable, not expecting much of an answer from the older man. The Sergeant was always somewhat reticent with answers to questions like that. Anything else would inspire the older copper to impart wisdom whether asked for or not, but never the drownings. If that's what they were. The constable was not sure he had the right of it. "Why would so many people come down to this damn village, dump their clothes and everything, then just walk into the sea?" he added, half to himself. It made no sense. Hell, there must be easier ways to off yourself. Ones that would save him picking up wet salty clothes from a beach that stunk of rotten seaweed. Always this damn stretch of beach as well.

The sergeant paused in his scrawling and looked at his younger colleague. Shook his head a moment and then went back to taking down the details.

"And why do we never get the bodies washing up? Tell me that," the youngster asked more himself than the sergeant who seemed to just accept this all as normal.

The sergeant's pencil nib broke, and he let out a sigh. Then looked up at his colleague once more. "It's like salmon, lad," he said, as if that explained everything.

"Sarge?"

"Alright, what's the one thing everyone knows about salmon, son?" the sergeant asked.

The constable, not it must be said a renowned thinker, thought for a moment before he answered. Then shrugged and went with the only thing he knew for sure about the fish. "They return to their spawning grounds to breed."

"Aye, well it's like that, I reckon."

"Sarge?"

"Salmon return from the sea and swim up the rivers to breed, right? Well, it's like that but what people forget, what they always forget, is that the salmon swim both ways. They swam down to the sea first, you see…" the sergeant told him.

"Er, yes, sarge, I guess, but I don't see what you're getting at," the constable said, and found himself looking out to sea, mildly captivated for a moment by the glint of sunlight off the crest of the waves.

The sergeant sighed again, and started strolling back to his patrol car, muttering to himself. "Nay, lad, you probably don't, but if you pull patrols around Dunwich long enough I dare say you will…"

Mark Hayes writes novels that often defy simple genre definitions; they could be described as speculative fiction, though Mark would never use the term as he prefers not to speculate. When not writing novels, Mark is a persistent pernicious procrastinator; he recently petitioned parliament for the removal of the sixteenth letter from the Latin alphabet. He is also 8th Dan Black Belt in the ancient Yorkshire martial art of EckEThump and favours a one man one vote system but has yet to supply the name of the man in question. Mark has also been known to not take writing his bio very seriously.

Find Mark on Twitter @darrackmark

•

Also by Mark Hayes

The Hannibal Smyth Misadventures:
A Scar of Avarice *novella
A Spider in the Eye
From Russia with Tassels
A Squid on the Shoulder (forthcoming)

The Ballad of Maybes series:
Maybe
Maybe's Daughter (forthcoming)

Passing Place
Cider Lane

Find out more at www.markhayesblog.com

FINCH

KATE BAUCHEREL

The weary traveller hoisted a heavy bag over one shoulder and slouched down the ramp into the spaceport. Unfamiliar sounds and smells assailed their senses, interrupted by the hiss of a disinfectant curtain and the regular sterile tang of chlorine. Shaking out a mess of wet feathers in disgust, they looked around for the nearest bar. A new planet? That called for a cocktail.

It was gloomy in the arrivals hall. Night had fallen, and this planet's paltry pair of moons were on the wane. There were very few other beings to be seen. Finch was surprised that no other passengers had made landfall from the ship, choosing instead to move on to the next stop in the traditional rite of passage round-the-galaxy trip. This wasn't the most popular destination on the circuit, but Finch was thorough. They wanted to see everything.

The roar of distant engines broke the silence. The ship was already departing; there was nothing to keep it here. Finch shrugged and moved on through the formalities of the small planetary customs post. They passed the identity scanners without a hitch and waited while a lackadaisical official poked around the pockets of their battered travelling bag.

"Thank you, Sir-Ma'am. On you go," said the guard.

Finch gave a shallow bow of thanks, retrieved the bag, and slung it back over their shoulder. Their feathers were still damp with chlorine and the strap of the bag itched. It was definitely time for a drink.

Outside the spaceport, the big, open town square was quiet but there were a few pockets of bright light and laughter to be found. Finch headed for a friendly-looking bar with tables outside and a crowd of locals enjoying the warm evening air. This place came highly recommended on the net reviews posted by other travellers, and the house cocktails were the stuff of legend. Inside, the bar was narrow and stretched far back into the depths of the building. The floor was covered in nutshells that had been casually discarded by drinkers, and Finch's feet, heavy in the higher gravity of this new planet, crunched loudly, causing a few heads to turn. Most of the customers ignored the new arrival, their attention focused on the octopod barman who was performing to his audience. His tentacles flashed around the shelves of spirits as he poured a dozen drinks at once. With a flourish he put the last bottles back in their places and reached for some bright local fruit to garnish the edges of each glass. Job done, he stepped back to rounds of applause. The two customers nearest the bar took a glass each and raised them in an appreciative toast, then moved away to let others through. Finch was borne forwards by the crowd, grinning broadly. This was exactly the way to celebrate a new destination. Finch reached for one of the last remaining drinks and raised the glass to the barman, catching his eye. Expecting a flash of smiling colour, Finch was surprised to see a sweep of cold hues across the barman's skin, gone as quickly as they came. A moment later the octopod's natural warm colours returned as the next customer took their drink. Finch shrugged. New planet, new people. It was hard to keep up with the body language of every species on this trip.

The drink was strong and sweet. Finch coughed at the first gulp, misjudging the strength of the vapours, but soon began to appreciate the heady mix of flavours and scents. The guides were right. This was one of the best cocktails in the galaxy. The volume of chatter in the bar had risen, and Finch was drawn into a friendly group of drinkers. The local language seemed easy to pick up and these new companions had a good level of intergalactic standard between them. The barman's tentacles whirled expertly and more drinks were delivered. It was shaping up to be a good evening, and if Finch wasn't careful, a forgettable one. However much fun it was, this would not do for the first time in an unfamiliar place. Time to find a bed for the night.

Finch sidled away from the laughing group and headed back to the bar. Service was slowing and the barman seemed to be taking a rest.

"Can I help you, stranger?" The barman was all smiles now, skin bathed in welcoming colours.

"Uh, yes," replied Finch. "I need to settle my tab, and I'm looking for a hostel if you can recommend one."

"Not leaving us, are you?" A woman approached and reached out to stroke Finch's iridescent black feathers. "Beautiful plumage," she said admiringly.

Finch had become used to this. Feathers were all the rage around the galaxy right now. Every couple of generations, avians found themselves on-trend as the fashions cycled and shifted. Finch shot a rueful glance at the barman and again saw the flash of cold colours. Disapproval? A warning? It was gone in a fraction of a second as he turned away to serve another customer.

The woman smiled. "I'm sure we can find you somewhere to stay, youngster. Here, join me for another drink." She gestured to the stool next to her.

"Thank you, no, I'd like to get some sleep," replied Finch politely. "If I can just settle up and you can point me in the right direction…?"

"Very well," shrugged the woman. She reached across the bar and expertly ripped a piece of paper off a spike. "This one's yours."

Finch took it, confused. The front was covered in scribbles from the bar, a tally of their drinks. The back was blank. There were no payment links to be seen. The material was plain, old-school paper, with no embedded chips to scan.

"Is there a wallet code, or do you have a transfer machine?" Finch asked.

"Local coins only," said the woman flatly. She nodded

towards the entrance where a poster stuck askew on the open door flapped in a light breeze. "Read the sign."

Another customer approached the bar and called for their tab. The barman reached out to the spike with a casual tentacle and handed over the drinker's tally. The customer laid a handful of coins on the bar and walked out with a cheery goodnight.

Finch's stomach churned, and it wasn't the drink. No planet used hard currency these days, and there had been no mention of this from the guides on the ship before they made planetfall. Pulling out their smart screen, Finch opened the familiar galactic standard payment app, but the software wouldn't load. No connection.

"No connection," confirmed the woman. "We went off-grid almost three months ago."

The bar had fallen silent, curious drinkers watching and waiting to see what happened next.

"What can I do?" stammered Finch, suddenly sober.

The woman stroked the soft feathers around Finch's tense shoulders. "I need some help here in the bar." She gestured at the nutshell-strewn floor. "My last avian cleaner is no longer with us. If you put in a good day's work tomorrow that should clear the debt. You'll stay here tonight." It was not an invitation, but an order.

The door closed with a firm click. The small room was at the top of the building, three flights up. It had been a hard climb with the planet's gravity pressing down on Finch's muscles, and despite being fit, they were tired. The grimy window should in theory have had a fine view out onto the square and the spaceport beyond, but the faint light of the moons had faded completely and there was nothing to see. The narrow bunk was hard, with a thin pillow and a thick blanket, neither promising much sleep through the warm and increasingly humid night. Finch sat sadly on a stool and disconsolately began to preen and tug at their feathers, head still spinning from the drinks. This was not a good start, but a day of hard work seemed a reasonable price to pay for those marvellous cocktails.

A sudden tap on the partly open window startled them. A familiar-looking tentacle wriggled its way through the crack and expertly popped the latch. It was followed by three more tentacles, then the top of the barman's head appeared.

"Hello youngster," he said gloomily. "Welcome to Petchinka."

"What...? Where...?" said Finch.

"I'm in the room next to you," said the barman. His skin flashed an indignant green. "I tried to warn you, but no, you went right ahead and walked into the trap."

"You didn't try very hard," protested Finch. "You served me three times."

"I flashed you. Should have been enough."

"I'm not that good at reading colours. I just thought you were being rude because I'm from out of town."

The barman scowled. "She was watching, wasn't she? She likes her avians, she does. I knew she'd have her eyes on you straight away, and she knew I knew." He shrugged with all three visible tentacles and wobbled slightly as his grip loosened on the window. "So, lad – you are going to be a lad, aren't you?"

Finch shook their head. "I don't know yet. I'm not ready to moult. Just call me Finch."

"The way you were putting back those cocktails, young Finch, I'd say you're leaning to male," said the barman, "but don't mind me, I'm just an old octopus."

Finch ignored the slight. Speculating on adult gender was frowned upon in polite avian circles, and cocktail consumption was hardly an indicator if the older nestlings in the family were anything to go by. The thought of family brought a lump to their throat.

"I need to contact my folks, let them know where I am."

"No chance of that, young Finch," said the barman. "No connection. Did no one warn you?"

Finch shook their head sadly, feathers drooping. "Is the whole planet off-grid? I wondered why no one else made planetfall. Odd, though. The tour guide recommended it. Surely they'd have known?"

"Depends," said the barman cautiously. "Were you the only avian on the ship?"

"Yes, just me," replied Finch. "Why?"

The barman's tentacles sagged and he lost his grip on the window. His head disappeared abruptly below the ledge for a moment. When he succeeded in pulling himself back up, his skin was a uniform dull grey which made Finch's blood run cold.

"I'm sorry," he said. "But there's nothing I can do." As quickly as he had arrived, he withdrew his tentacles and vanished from sight.

"Wait!" shouted Finch.

There was a gentle slithering sound as the barman slipped back into his own window, then silence.

Finch glanced fearfully at the door, but no one had heard the shout. What had they wandered into? Thinking quickly, they emptied their travelling bag onto the bed. Buried under the debris of three months on the circuit and landfall on half a dozen worlds was an old printed guidebook that their grandmother had forced on them as a farewell gift. What had she said? *"This was the galaxy I visited at your age, Finch. Let me know how much it's changed."*

What had changed, and what had stayed the same? Flicking through the yellowed pages, Finch was soon absorbed in the archaic language and outlandish descriptions of places they had already passed and places they planned to go. Judging by ticket stubs folded into the pages and notes in the margin in a confident hand, Granny had followed a very similar itinerary. Despite the desperate situation, Finch lingered over old pictures of the last planet they'd visited. In Granny's day, it had been a desert of glass and concrete, proud at the peak of its commercial powers. Now it was a softer place where nature had taken over. Finch longed to be back there, white water rafting through a canyon of half-drowned skyscrapers and eating in treetop canopy restaurants with young travellers from all across the galaxy. It was a far cry from this hellhole.

Ah. There it was. The guidebook entry for this current planet was crossed through. Granny had not made landfall. Finch took a deep breath and started to read.

Planet: Petchinka. Location: Polaris Goldilocks zone. Moons: two. Rotation: 20 standard hours. Orbit: 290 days. Climate: Largely temperate to tropical, cooler at poles. Natural resources: diamonds, lesser gemstones, copper. Galactic exports: high-end luxury goods and clothing.

Finch frowned, confused. When they'd been researching for this trip, all the articles about Petchinka talked of the planet's thriving tourist industry, its admittedly fabulous cocktails, and the not-to-be missed spectacle of the diamond waterfall a day's ride from the main spaceport. There had been no mention of any galactic-scale industry. Finch picked up their smartscreen without thinking, but of course there was no signal, no way of searching for more. They sighed. Nothing could be done before the morning. Time to get some sleep.

Shafts of light from the rising sun penetrated the grubby window, dazzling Finch's drowsy eyes, and the sound of rocket engines brought a good hangover into sharp focus. Groaning, Finch struggled upright to look at the view. The spaceport was across the square and a ship was just departing into the upper atmosphere. That explained the noise. A few small, battered container ships were waiting on the pad amid a bustle of activity. Finch frowned. The spaceport should be buzzing with tourists, not cargo.

Something caught Finch's eye, and it took a moment for them to realise why. The spaceport comms tower. Of course. There had to be a signal for the interplanetary traffic that came and went daily. Petchinka was not completely off the grid after all. Looking around the square, Finch spotted more network masts nestling among the rooftops. Domestic connections may be down, but the infrastructure was still there.

Feeling a little more hopeful, Finch preened a few feathers and turned away from the window. The guidebook lay on the floor where it had fallen the previous night. Finch picked it up and found the page they'd been reading.

"Petchinkan luxury goods: the jewellery from this planet is highly prized. Diamonds are of exceptional quality, although the native copper settings do not suit the taste of every market. Copper jewellery is specifically not advised for electric species with highly conductive skin. Provenanced diamonds are also supplied for cutting and setting off-world. Clothing manufacture encompasses a full range from copycat fast fashion to the manufacture of catwalk collections."

Finch was puzzled. This guidebook was less than a century old. How could a world have changed its entire focus in the space of three generations? They read on.

"Concerns have been raised at the galactic council over worker conditions and the sourcing of raw materials. Tourists are asked to exercise caution. The advice to av…"

The door flew open and Finch hurriedly dropped the book. The hostess from the bar stood in the doorway, arms folded.

"Are you ready to do some work, youngster?" She ushered Finch out, closed the door, and gestured towards the narrow stairs. "There's plenty to tidy up from last night, and a lot of washing up for you to do." She stroked the fine feathers on Finch's back. "You're not the first traveller to let a few drinks scupper your plans, and you won't be the last."

"How long do you need me for?" asked Finch hesitantly. "Just today? I wanted to see the diamond waterfall, and the tour guide on the ship booked me on a caravan which leaves tomorrow morning."

"We'll see," replied the woman. "I'm sure this will be the only day you have to work."

Reassured, Finch relaxed as they reached the bottom of the stairs, but the sight of the bar made them groan. There were dirty glasses everywhere, discarded garnish crushed into the layer of nutshells on the floor, and a pervasive stench of whatever weed the locals had been smoking after Finch went to bed. There was a full day's cleaning here, for sure. The woman smiled and handed them a bucket and cloth.

"All yours," she said.

Finch scrubbed and washed and swept until their back ached. From time to time, the woman appeared, nodded, and disappeared back up the stairs to her office. Once or twice visitors came through the bar to see her. They were all drawn to Finch's feathers, stroking them in passing. It was increasingly annoying, but Finch held their tongue. No use getting into more trouble. The diamond waterfall was waiting, and then they could get off this lousy planet and pick up on the tour itinerary again.

It was mid-afternoon by the time Finch finished cleaning. A couple of customers were already sitting outside in the sunshine, waiting for the door to open. The barman slouched down the stairs and waved a tentacle towards the exhausted avian.

"Nice work, young Finch," he said. "Very impressive. I didn't know the floor was that colour underneath all the nutshells." His skin glowed a contented pink and he slipped into his place behind the bar.

"Yes, that's excellent." The woman emerged from the stairwell and gave Finch a wide smile. "Why don't you go and rest? You'll be tired. I'll send up some food."

Finch didn't argue. Back aching, they clambered wearily up the three flights of stairs and flung themselves on the narrow bed. Sleep came quickly.

It was already dark when Finch woke. The sound of laughter wafted through the open window from drinkers who had spilled out onto the square. Another good night was in progress. Finch stood up and ruffled their feathers, stretching. Despite everything, the hard work had helped them to sleep well. Opening the door, Finch found a tray of food waiting as promised. No cocktail to accompany it, though. That had been too much to hope for. Digging into the admittedly delicious hotpot, Finch began to feel stronger. Looking around the room, they noticed it had been tidied. The scattered contents of the travelling bag had been carefully collected on a shelf, including the precious guidebook. Feathers that Finch had let fall to the floor after preening were gone. This wasn't so bad. They'd just been a little incautious on their first day on a new planet. A good night's rest and they'd be off to the diamond waterfalls in the morning.

Finch put the empty tray carefully back outside the door and settled down as comfortably as possible, guidebook in hand. They flicked through a few more old photographs and notes, amused and touched at the glimpse into Granny's youth. Finch reflected on the life she'd had, evolving from a youthful traveller to a benevolent matriarch loved by all the nestlings. Was that the direction Finch would take when the time came?

Turning again to the entry for Petchinka, Finch was brought up short. "Tourists are asked to exercise caution. The advice to avians remains unchanged: all but essential travel to the planet should be avoided."

Finch turned the page, shocked, but there was no more detail to be found. The guidebook moved on to the delights of the next planet on the galactic itinerary, once again annotated by their grandmother. Finch made a fruitless search of the index for any further mention of Petchinka, fumbling in their haste. The book fell to the ground, photographs and mementoes spilling from it. Fighting back tears, Finch bent to gather the scattered papers up, trying to fit them into the right pages, making the book whole again.

On a slip of delicate close-printed paper, the word Petchinka caught Finch's eye. Unfolding it carefully, Finch found a news article. "Avian citizens warned after third disappearance." Dated almost a century earlier, the story was simple but horrifying. A handful of visitors to the planet – this planet – had failed to contact their families after landfall and had not been seen since.

A tap on the window made Finch jump out of his skin. A pink tentacle appeared, then the barman's eyes.

"I'm finished for the night. How are you doing, youngster?" He frowned, seeing Finch's distress. "Are you alright?"

"What do you know?" demanded Finch without preamble. "What's happened here?"

The barman's skin flashed a complex pattern of colours. "What do you mean?" he asked innocently.

"You apologised to me last night. You tried to warn me about something. What? Do you know anything about the history of this place?"

"You've guessed, then," sighed the octopod. "They need the feathers."

"I thought that was it. But they won't get many feathers off a preening juvenile, and it'll be another few years before I moult…"

Finch looked up and met the barman's gaze. There was only one other way to harvest avian plumage.

"What happened to the old cleaner?"

The octopod froze at the window, turning a deep, horrified red. His eyes widened.

"They disappeared. I thought they'd moulted and left, and she'd collected the feathers."

"Moulting isn't that straightforward," said Finch frantically. "It takes weeks. I need to get out of here."

"I'm sorry," said the barman. "Truly I am. I'll help you any way I can."

Finch's breathing settled, thoughts clearing. "Okay. I have to get a message out to the authorities and tell my folks where I am. Is there a mast on this roof?"

"Yes," said the barman.

"That's where we're going, then. It can't be hard to relay a signal to the spaceport tower."

"How do you plan to get up there, youngster?"

Finch smiled faintly. "I may not be able to fly, but I can climb."

Picking up the smartscreen, Finch tucked it into a discreet under-arm pocket pouch. The window was small but they should just fit. Peering up the face of the building, Finch was relieved that it seemed to be a short climb to the roof. The moons had set and the town was cloaked in darkness. Their dark plumage was perfect camouflage.

"Right. You're my safety gear. First, can you pull the frame out of this window – quietly!"

The octopod obediently wrapped a tentacle around the cross-piece and pulled. The woodwork gave way easily. On closer inspection, it was rotting in places. That would be a useful alibi if the plan went wrong, thought Finch.

"Okay. I'm coming out. I need you to give me footholds and handholds all the way up. Can you do that?"

"Sure, kiddo." Clinging firmly to tiny cracks and overhangs in the stonework, he set four tentacles in place. Finch squeezed out of the window, trying hard not to look down, and reached for the first hold. So far so good. Now for the real test. Finch stood wobbling on the windowsill and tentatively reached out a claw to the foothold.

"Ouch!" complained the barman in a strained whisper. To his credit the tentacle holding Finch's weight stayed firm.

Spreadeagled on the face of the building, Finch breathed steadily. "Let's go."

As Finch lifted each limb, the octopod crawled up the stonework and provided new holds. They moved sinuously together up to the top of the wall and disappeared over the edge of the roof. Lying quietly, breathing heavily, Finch listened. There were no shouts or alarms. They hadn't been spotted. So far, so good.

The mast was at the highest point of the gently sloping roof. Finch crawled up and examined it carefully. The main structure looked to be intact, but in the light of the smartscreen Finch spotted some broken connections and a few surprisingly familiar-looking traces on the metal.

"Sucker marks! Did you have something to do with this?"

The octopod looked embarrassed. "I'm as much of a

prisoner as you, youngster, but I have a good life here. I helped them to disable the network but this should be easy enough to fix." He undulated towards the mast and picked up some of the trailing wires. "It's just a question of putting these back in place."

His tentacles flew around expertly, tucking frayed cables into place and twisting broken ends together by the dim light of the smartscreen. Finch kept tapping to pick up a connection.

"How's that?"

"Nothing yet."

"Hmm." More wires, more adjustments. "Now?"

"Nothing… Wait! Yes!" Finch suppressed a whoop of relief. "I'm connected to the main net. I'm just waiting for the services to load." They tapped an impatient claw on the roof. "This is so slow."

"You're in, that's the main thing. Now, they'll notice pretty quickly that this thing is back online. Get your messages sent, youngster."

Finch tapped urgently at the screen. "I've sent an SOS to the galactic police, and a message to my mum."

"That'll do. You don't need me any more, then."

"What? Aren't you trying to get away too?"

"Ah, young Finch. It's more complicated than you think. I don't want the galactic police breathing down my neck. I'd appreciate it if you don't mention me when they rescue you."

"What do you mean?"

"I've had a colourful life," replied the barman, "and

there are a few people who seem to think that I did them wrong. I'm content that I've done right by you, and I don't want to do time in a galactic jail for old crimes. I need to be away from here before the cavalry turns up. I don't want anyone to get wind of this evening's adventures."

"Thank you, from the bottom of my heart," said Finch. "Of course I'll help. What do you need me to do?"

"Easy enough," said the barman. He clambered onto the mast and took hold of it with the end of two tentacles. "Pull me back, aim over there," he pointed at a barely visible white patch, a distant rooftop, "and let me go. And wipe off those sucker marks."

Finch smiled and carefully gathered up the old octopod, pulling until the two tentacles were stretched to their furthest extension.

"Now," he said. Finch released their grip and the octopod catapulted through the air, multicoloured skin flashing. As he disappeared into the dark, there was a faint cry. "Good luck, youngster."

For a few moments, Finch sat in darkness and silence. Suddenly the smartscreen lit up with alerts, and shouts came from the square below. High in the sky a bright light had appeared and was approaching the planet at speed. The cavalry had arrived.

As the police cruiser decelerated sharply and settled into high altitude orbit, powerful searchlights blazed. Across the square on the edge of a white roof, a grateful tentacle waved briefly before sliding off into shadow.

Finch stood up and signalled frantically at the swarm of drones released by the cruiser. It was time to leave.

•

A sci fi fan since first seeing the Daleks from behind the sofa, Kate Baucherel works on the application of new and emerging technologies to solve business problems. Sometimes her imagination gets the better of her, and the tech of the fictional worlds in her writing is rooted in the possibilities already at our fingertips. Her work includes the SimCavalier futurist cybercrime series, several short stories, and non-fiction books for business leaders. The opening lines of Finch were originally published in her 2020 book on blockchain and cryptocurrency, Blockchain Hurricane.

Also by Kate Baucherel

The SimCavalier Trilogy:
Bitcoin Hurricane (2017)
Hacked Future (2018)
Tangled Fortunes (due 2020)

Short stories:
Gridlock (2019)
White Christmas (2019)

Poles Apart: Challenges for business in the Digital Age
(MX Publishing, 2014)

Blockchain Hurricane: Origins, Applications and Future of Blockchain and Cryptocurrency (Business Expert Press, 2020)

Find out more at katebaucherel.com

THE BEAST

ADRIAN BAGLEY

Beast shifted in the darkness, chains chinking softly as he rubbed at aching wrists. He had long since outgrown the manacles that bound him, but the Masters did not care. He was beneath their notice, a beast fit only to be kept in the stables with the other animals.

But he was patient, and he had a plan.

All his life he had known nothing but the shackle and the whip. By night he slept with the horses, by day he toiled for the Masters among the lofty heights of Eldanheir, greatest and most ancient of the timeless cities of the elves. Not that any elf would deign to instruct him – he was their slaves' slave, working for human house-thralls trusted to manage the day-to-day needs of the Masters.

Only the most menial and back-breaking of tasks were his, and he took pride in that, for none could bear the loads he could lift, nor labour as long as he. He worked without complaint. He climbed the highest branches, crossed the most precarious of spans, cleaned the foulest of waste, and uttered no word of protest. He served in obedient silence. And he *hated*.

He hated the elves. He hated the humans, who were

no freer than he but beat him as readily as any overseer. He hated glorious, painfully beautiful Eldanheir with its sculpted boughs, its soaring bridges and spans of greenwood, its treetop palaces and aerial gardens. So many wild things tamed by the elves and made to serve their needs, just as he was.

The elves called this *imbrahil*. The closest human word would be 'civilisation', but to the elves it meant much more: order, beauty, tradition – all that the elf lords valued, and sought to impose on the tribes of primitive men and urech who roamed the surrounding plains. From time to time he would hear tell of a distant battle, and a fresh flood of human slaves would enter the city. His own people were rarely taken, since they could not be trained – unless, as he had been, they were found as infants and raised in servitude. When elf fought urech it was not to enslave, but to exterminate.

A glimmer of light through the stable doors spoke of approaching dawn, and Beast drew himself up to his full height, waiting patiently. It was not long before the doors swung back and a diminutive figure stepped through, unlocking the heavy chain that leashed his leg to the wall.

"Good morrow, Yonas."

"Beast."

He had known no other name in all his days. He was Beast, the lowest of the low, with no more status in Eldanheir than a stray dog.

"We'll be working in the distillery again," Yonas announced cheerfully, ignoring his sour look. "Third time this week the pipes have clogged. They'll want the whole thing taken down and cleaned, I expect. Maybe we'll get to sneak some fine elven brandy while no one's looking." He grinned.

Beast grimaced and spat. "I tried that once. Their wine is sickeningly sweet, but their spirits are worse. More treacle than plum. I'd rather give it to the horses and drink what comes out."

Yonas laughed. "To each his own, eh?" The lad looked at him, suddenly serious. "You going to escape, Beast?"

"If I was, I wouldn't tell you."

"That's what you always say. You aren't the only one who dreams of freedom, you know. We could meet, make plans."

Beast snorted. "I don't trust your friends. I'm not sure I trust you, come to that."

Yonas scowled. "I'm the only one who even talks to you. You won't make it alone. Even if you escape, they'll hunt you down. They kill runaways, no second chances."

"Then don't run away."

Yonas threw up his hands. "Have it your way! Come on, I don't want to be beaten for tardiness."

Beast's wide nostrils flared as he stepped into the morning light, mouth gaping as he tasted the dawn. The stench of elf was faint here at the foot of the arboreal city. He was surrounded by trees ten times as wide as he stood tall, each rising from a clearing of trimmed grass and carefully cultivated spring flowers. The beginnings of a northerly breeze brought with it the earthy musk of deer and rabbit, of wolf and kestrel and a dozen other creatures that scuttled and loped, burrowed and flew among the mighty trees.

He let out a low growl as his stomach clenched, and saliva dripped between his fangs.

"Easy," Yonas said from behind him. "No food until we work for it, you know that."

Beast said nothing. He could run now, take a horse and be away before the sun cleared the horizon. Elven arrows would fill his back long before he reached the edge of the city. Just because their scent was faint, did not mean they were not there, watching the forest floor for enemies – aye, and runaways like him. He closed his mouth and stood straighter; let them see him walk proudly to his work, not cowed like an over-whipped cur.

Not far from the stable lay a curiously shaped tree, one of many that, by means Beast could not imagine, the elves had persuaded to grow at an angle to the ground, and whose bark sported (apparently quite naturally) a series of ridges forming a steep but manageable stair. Bowers of sweet-smelling flowers arched above the flight in hues of lake blue and honey gold, while soft moss carpeted each step. Exotic birds perched among the flowers, paying man and urech no heed, but singing for the dawn in perfect harmony – a true dawn chorus, jarringly false to Beast's primal sensibilities. Once, he had snatched a bird to sate his hunger. He bore the scars of his punishment still, beside those of many others.

Up the strange stair clambered Beast, muscles bunching under skin the colour of weathered granite. Yonas followed, puffing and complaining at the pace.

"Why do you hurry so?" the lad called plaintively. "Are you eager for the day's toil?"

Beast tossed back his head and laughed, red-black hair streaming out behind him. "We must not keep the Masters waiting!" he cried as he sped upwards.

Yonas moaned and scrambled after him.

A hundred feet above the ground, the incline became more shallow, the tree trunk bowing until it was almost horizontal, before rearing up to the vertical and exploding in a great tangle of leaves and branches, as if to make up for the lack of these below. Here, where the slope was at its most shallow, the tree came to rest against a gargantuan oak, so that it was clear the one had been grown to provide access to the upper reaches of the other.

All around the vast girth of the oak, the elves had constructed a platform, not of planks, but of woven living branches, supported by sturdier boughs that rose like buttresses from the bole. On every side, nestled among colossal beeches, elms, ashes and alders, platforms sprouted from the forest canopy. Upon each rose dwellings great and small, garlanded in flowers and verdant leaves. Every inch of the city teemed with beauty and life, swaying disconcertingly in the rising wind.

Beast mounted the platform, and from its height gazed upon the forest and all its marvels. He hated it, not for its beauty but for its rotten heart. That something so exquisite should be founded on drudgery stirred a profound resentment within him. Was the forest not splendid enough? Did every flower need its own slave in order to bloom? Everything here was false, tailored and transplanted, crafted in pain to serve the whims of the Masters. That the result was undeniably wondrous only made his outrage worse, as if his own eyes betrayed him.

Yonas' head appeared through the hatch behind him, and Beast reached down a meaty hand to heft the lad through. It was a short distance to the distillery, past gardens of miniature trees planted among the branches of their giant relatives, aviaries flaunting birds in a rainbow of colours, displays of flowers found nowhere in nature for a hundred leagues or more; all painstakingly wrought and lovely beyond measure, yet serving no practical purpose Beast could discern. Elves did not labour to rear livestock or cultivate their own crops, they raised songbirds and planted flower beds, and left baser matters to their thralls.

Despite his bitterness, Beast strode to the distillery with a spring in his step, and flung open its door almost joyfully.

"You are late."

A group of elves were lounging among three great wooden vats – each twice the height of a tall man, connected to a tangled maze of glass piping and heated from below by smoky brass stoves. They had clearly been sampling their own product, though they showed few of the usual signs. Elves were nigh immune to the effects of alcohol – almost, but not quite, a technicality they exploited to the full. They drank hard liquor as any other race would quaff ale, becoming ever merrier but rarely intoxicated. Each bore a slim rapier strapped to his or her waist, and each would be expert in its use. Fickle as they were, elves were passionate in their hobbies, and thought nothing of spending a decade or more frenziedly practising the art of swordplay, until some other pastime caught their eye.

The door slammed behind Beast and Yonas, caught by a sudden gust. Yonas apologised hastily.

"Forgive our slowness, Masters, and our clumsiness."

The elf huffed theatrically. "I suppose you cannot help your deficiencies. Be more careful in future." The floor rocked, and she glanced out of a window woven into the wall. "There will be a storm today, I fancy."

Beast grinned savagely. The elves of Eldanheir were renowned for their weather lore, and this was just the augury he would have wished for.

"Be about your work, then. The pipes are clogged again. I fear you will have to clean the vats, but inspect them first, before we are forced to discard the whole batch."

Beast bowed his assent and opened a tap low down on the side of the first vat, catching the liquid in a wooden cup. He tilted it this way and that, examining the consistency of the plum mush as it slopped against the side of the cup.

"Here, lad," he called to Yonas, who was inspecting the intricate pipework for blockages. "Fetch me those steps and I'll open the lid to see what's what."

Yonas obliged, manoeuvring the stepladder into position beside the vat. Beast bounded up the first few rungs, before patting the side of the vat thoughtfully, a broad grin on his mottled features.

One of the elves, a tall fellow who near matched Beast's own considerable height, noticed his expression and regarded him haughtily.

"You, slave – always you are grim and sullen, yet today your heart seems light and full of good cheer. Whence come these high spirits?"

Beast laughed, his heart light indeed, and gripped the huge vat in brawny arms.

"Today you will grant my freedom," he called down, "or all Eldanheir will burn!"

The elves gasped at this insolence, and the tall one drew his sword. "Come down from there at once," he cried. "Apologise, or we will have you flogged."

Beast only grinned at him, lips spread wide over a mouthful of ivory fangs. Bracing his legs and straining every sinew, he heaved against the vat and sent it crashing down. Glassware snapped, and then smashed as the vat plunged through it, spilling raw mash and fiery liquor throughout the room.

With a single bound, Beast was at the door. As the stunned elves watched in horror, he reached into his belt, plucked out an earthenware fire pot, and brandished it with a flourish.

Yonas caught his eye, standing terrified among the ruined pipework, and Beast hesitated. Seizing the lad's arm, he hauled him clear and thrust him roughly through the door. As the elves howled and rushed forward, he dashed the pot to the ground and dived after the boy.

There was a dull whump as the alcohol caught. Flames shot from the doorway, singeing the back of Beast's tunic and setting his hair ablaze. Frantically, he patted it out with leathery hands, twisting to look back at the burning building. Screams faded into the hiss and crackle of the flames.

Quickly, he dragged Yonas to his feet and made for the hatch and the stairway down, reaching it just as a mighty detonation resounded from the distillery. The fire had reached the stockpile of brandy barrels and caused them to explode, blasting through the south wall and showering burning liquid onto nearby buildings.

Beast fled through the hatch, cannoning into a startled elf with such force that the fellow was knocked clean from the stair. Yonas gaped as the Master fell with a high-pitched scream, striking the ground far below.

Down the steps they flew, torn and buffeted by the rising gale. Beast leapt from stair to stair, sure-footed as any animal, while Yonas slipped and stumbled along behind as best he could; and as they went, Beast cried out in a booming voice,

"Fire! Fire! Bring water ere all Eldanheir burns!"

Again and again he called, and if any elf saw him, they thought only of the need to douse the flames before their city was lost, and nothing of the motives of a pair of hurrying slaves.

Beast dropped the last dozen feet to the ground and sped to the stable doors. The horses had long since grown accustomed to their strange stable-mate, and whickered a greeting as he entered. He made for a black stallion, his favourite, tall, strong and proud. Often he had saved some morsel too sweet for his own palette as a gift for the animal, and it made no fuss now as Beast vaulted to its back. He was glad, since there was no time for a saddle, and he had no more knowledge of riding than could be gleaned from trotting the creature the length of the stable in the dead of night when some kindly human had neglected to shackle him.

Yonas staggered in after him, puffing with exertion, and Beast swung the boy up behind him. He wavered a moment, almost losing his seat, before steadying himself and prodding the stallion into the open with a gentle dig of his heels.

"'Ware!" he cried into the teeth of the gale. "Fire sweeps the city!"

He did not exaggerate. Driven by the strong north wind, flames had spread through the branches high above them, leaping from building to building, bough to bough, growing ever fiercer as they went. Wheeling his mount, Beast spurred the creature north and west, as sparks and blackened foliage rained in hissing torrents around them.

One great branch came crashing down in front of the stallion and it reared in fright, nearly unseating its novice riders. Beast lurched precariously, clinging on by the strength of his huge legs alone, squeezing so hard that the horse wheezed and almost foundered.

Yonas had his arms tight about Beast's chest, holding on for dear life. "Such a price," he wept, staring wild-eyed at the blaze. "Must so much be lost for the sake of our freedom?"

Beast grunted. "You still think the city beautiful." He shook his head sadly. "Beauty exists to serve man, not the other way about. Each bud of this forest is soiled by the crack of whip against flesh, poisoned by the blood of broken men. There is no uglier place in all the world."

He did not allow the pace to slacken until they had cleared the blaze. Then he turned and rode hard across the northern fringe of the fire, watching as it swept the canopy above, swelling into a mighty conflagration as it was blown ever southward. Even the famed magic of the elves would not stop such an inferno.

"Eldanheir is lost!" he cried, fighting to keep the joy from his voice. "Flee! Flee the city! 'Ware the bane of the elves!"

He drove the stallion harder, tasting freedom now; but the horse, maddened by smoke and the crackle of flames, reared a second time and the pair were thrown.

Beast managed to roll as he struck the ground, coming to his feet with no worse injury than a painful bruise. Yonas did not rise, lying still with his head at a curious angle.

Beast cursed, all gladness gone from him. "Such a

price," he said mournfully. Bile arose in his throat and he choked on the bitter taste of it.

The stallion was backing away, eyes rolling, foam flecking its mouth. Before he could move towards the creature, a lithe form dropped from above, landing smoothly atop its back. The horse bucked and kicked at thin air, but the elf called strange words in a honeyed tone and it calmed, tossing its head and breathing deeply.

"Never have I seen a horse handled so poorly," the elf said, fixing Beast with a glare.

He noted the bow slung across the elf's shoulder, and measured the distance between them.

"Small wonder your companion lies dead," the other continued dismissively. "No matter; I will take his worth from your hide later. For now, you will stop this foolish galloping and join the effort to douse the fire."

Beast bowed his assent meekly, and moved as if to remount the stallion. The elf kicked him away.

"I will take the horse, dolt! You have caused enough harm."

Beast pounced. The elf started, reaching for his belt dagger, but Beast's hands closed about his neck. Momentum carried them both to the ground and there was a sharp crack. The breath left Beast's lungs, his head struck something hard, and the world went black.

He did not know how long he lay there. He was roused by a terrible pounding in his temples, and the smell of blood. *His* blood, seeping from a wound in the side of his head. He pushed himself groggily off the root he had struck and staggered to his feet. The stallion was passively cropping the grass nearby, its fears forgotten. The elf lay motionless where he had fallen.

Beast prodded the lifeless form with one toe. Satisfied, he seized the horse by its mane and rolled onto its back, gasping at a sudden wave of nausea. Gingerly, he eased the creature to a trot. He shook his shaggy head, trying to clear the darkness from his vision, and growled softly to himself. This was no time for weakness.

He was not certain how long he rode thus, aimless and half-insensible, but the instincts of the stallion served him well. He raised his head to find they were clear of the city, riding through wild forest unsullied by the hand of man or elf. A great pall of smoke blotted out the sky behind.

It would rain soon, when the brewing storm finally broke, and perhaps the fires would be quenched. Beast did not care. Free air filled his lungs, and for the first time in his life the shadow of the whip did not haunt him. Before his horse's hooves lay miles of forest he had never seen, and then hills and plains populated by tribes of men and urech who had never tasted captivity. An untamed world to explore and savour.

He threw back his head and bellowed with delight. *Freedom!*

Adrian Bagley is a writer from the south coast of England. He is currently working on his debut science fiction novel, Case in Point. He writes serious and humorous fiction in a variety of styles, matching the prose to the needs of the story.

He has severe ME, which he combats with a strict regimen of blaspheming and coffee.

Find out more at
www.facebook.com/adrianbagleywriter/

SEEDS

ANDREW OPENSHAW

Excitement for tomorrow's festival was keeping Ada awake. She wanted to hear stories of when the land here was different. So, we walked until we came to a dip in the ground and I realised this was an old ditch. It reminded me of Nicola again and the events of eight years ago. I got Ada settled and built a fire.

•

After digging the ditch, I had started back to the tents, eager to warm my hands and eat. Nicola continued giving orders, urging the others to hurry else it'd be nightfall and the wolves would start circling. Eri waved, and distracted, I tripped on a length of piping. Her laughter quickened my pace until my boots reached sturdy soil. She tried standing as I entered the camp, but I ushered her down and leaned in, rubbing her nose with mine, my hand immediately resting on her stomach. We sat as the children played until a warning call brought everyone through the gates, dumping shovels and grabbing rifles. I stood again on weary legs and helped Eri inside.

The travellers had ragged beards lined with snow and raw eyes which spoke of endless wandering. Thankfully none were sick, and Nicola set our cooks to work, though some grumbled at the apparent lack of gratitude shown. An urgency to their expedition meant the men soon moved on, much to our relief, and people returned to their tasks. Everyone but Nicola. I found her at the north gate, staring into the oncoming blizzard. Ten years she'd spent here, helping us build a home and better understand the land, but we always knew part of her was somewhere else.

"Nicola," I said. "They're not our concern now. Don't worry."

Without turning, she replied, "Prepare the sledges and find Leif and Lasse. Tell them we need a month's worth of food and supplies."

When I demanded reasons for this unexpected flight, she said, "Those men have a key."

And within a few hours, we were on our way.

•

The bear's blood marked a crimson line across the snow. I fired again, and the beast howled and spun back, rearing up to its full seven feet, a dark patch spoiling its brilliant white fur around the mouth and nose. When I reloaded and took aim, it recognised what was coming, dropped down and started retreating. My shaking hands struggled to discharge the weapon, its pop like the sickening crack of Lasse's skull.

Nicola dug frantically, trying to hide the worst it, but when my crunching boots joined the slicing shovel, she gave up and buried her head in her hands. I joined her next to the grave and we wept together, the tears stinging my face with each gust of wind.

Together we dragged Leif's corpse back to the tents. He and Lasse now lay side by side, their mutilated faces pointing at clear blue skies, the earth beneath them like a burnt hole. Nicola told me to gather the materials scattered around. We were only a mile or so away from the boat and the storm had eased considerably overnight, but she remained resolute. So, we buried them and got ready to move on.

•

The snow became softer the further we got from the coast, and with each step, the top of our thighs ached. But with determination, we covered several miles across the glaringly white landscape. Those first few hours after burying Leif and Lasse, the pace was driven by fear. Whatever buoyancy had got us to the port and across the sea during those unremarkable two weeks, turned into despair and grief-ridden stomping.

I needed a break, but Nicola urged us on. She even took the burden of our sledge for long periods, letting me lift my head up and enjoy the sun on my face. We spoke occasionally, which I appreciated, as I had many unanswered questions about the journey ahead. But whenever my curiosity piqued, Nicola would shut down, leaving the crunching snow to fill the empty white silence.

An hour later, the sun had retreated into the skyline. The wind stopped teasing a storm, and heavy snow started falling. Nicola paused and pressed her hood up to mine. We started kicking the toes of each other's boots and blinking off the ice.

"Camp here?" I said.

"No."

She retrieved a small black box from her coat, with a single red light blinking on its surface. When she pushed her padded thumb onto it, the light went away. "Five miles," she said. Beyond her, the smooth unbroken landscape persisted.

After two miles, my momentum ground to a halt. I waved my arms around and moaned through the layers, but Nicola didn't respond. The hush wrapped itself around me, bringing with it a sickly chill.

The sky bloomed, wild purples melting into brilliant oranges and reds. My body, right up from my legs to my head, began pouring away along with the paint pot sky. Pleasant dreams passed through me, of cooking smells and comforting chatter, blazing fires and fertile lands. I thought of my father, me shaking him, screaming for him to break his trance, but him, stiff as bone, refusing to blink and acknowledge I was there. His tortured days stuck reliving a world that no longer existed, refusing to accept that everything he'd worked for was gone.

•

Something was shaking me, and when I opened my eyes, Nicola placed a hand on my face and smiled, though her dark eyes had a sadness I had yet to understand. When I crawled from the tent, she stood monitoring the white plains, making sure we were alone. As she crunched down to adjust her boot, her hair hiding her face, I saw it for the first time – a dull asphalt block, with a silvery surface reflecting the sun.

We packed everything away and stood side by side, gazing warily at the structure. The sky was darker now, deeper hues of blue and grey. I wanted to lie down again and enjoy the tent's insulation, but Nicola was ready. She started into a jog, as I followed, glancing around for the men we'd tracked here. Further up the hill, more of the structure became visible. Sturdy black windowless boxes set into the landscape.

"Are they here?" I said when I sidled up to her.

Her gloved hand explored the rough edges, confirming they were real. Out came her blinking box again. She nodded and tucked it back in her coat.

"It's open?"

"Yes, come on."

•

Inside, we passed several doors. Nicola didn't acknowledge them, whereas I touched each one, curious about what they contained. The winding corridors emerged into a large living area with a table and chairs. Dozens of decaying mattresses covered the floor and an old computer screen and keyboard sat on a desk in the corner. I'd seen one of these as a child, poking around the abandoned houses. We'd dared each other to press the keys to see if we could coax it back to life, but it remained inanimate, so we each spat on the screen and ran back outside.

The tunnel continued into the mountain and we passed through three identical doors left open by the men. When we approached the final main access door, a loud crash echoed around the tunnel. I started to speak, but Nicola forced her finger over my mouth, her eyes wide and pleading. Laughter came from the room nearest our position, and footsteps approached but moved quickly past. Voices chattered until the group recovered what had fallen and returned to their separate rooms.

In the main vault, the men had illuminated the space. Passing through the door was like entering a womb-like structure. Vivid glistening frost coated the walls, a multitude of twinkling particles reaching all the way to the roof. Nicola's firm hand pulled me behind some stacked boxes at the side of the room.

She swiped at her box, revealing four lights dispersed across a screen.

"Hey!" came a voice, and a figure appeared in a side doorway. Pretty soon, all four men had emerged and closed in around us, shouting and raising their arms.

We stepped from behind our cover to face the group, hands up at our shoulders.

"We only want to talk. Come to an arrangement," Nicola shouted above them. "The seeds here belong to everyone."

"How the hell did you get here?" said one of the men.

"You're not supposed to be here," said another. "Get them."

"Wait, " said Nicola as she stepped back towards the wall. "Wait a second."

My heart hammered in my chest, my fingers tingling at the ends. We shuffled back, and the four crept closer, ready to jump us.

"We fed you, helped you on your way," pleaded Nicola. "Share the spoils, it's not much to ask."

The first man who spoke, the oldest of the four, stepped forward and glared at us. "You played your part and your story will be recorded in the histories, but your narrative ends here. A new chapter is beginning, and his hand has not written you into the next part of the tale."

That was all Nicola needed. She gave me a shove and I fell, disappearing under a heap of boxes. Four gunshots rang out in quick succession, followed by a series of thuds. A body landed on the pile and I pushed it off, my head emerging from the cover of cardboard and foil packets. Blood on the concrete reached as far as Nicola's boots. I gazed up at her, slack-jawed.

"Where...?" I started to ask.

Footsteps echoed from the corridor. I ducked back undercover as his gun went off. Nicola dropped to the floor, her scream echoing around the room. Peering through a gap, I saw the fifth man point his rifle at her, as she held her stomach with bloody hands.

"Fuck!" he yelled. "You are not part of his plan!" He started walking over to where Nicola lay. "Chaos rained down upon this world to cleanse it of unbelievers like you. What life do you have here? You're clinging on for nothing when the gates of heaven stay open awaiting your return. Accept him into your heart now and die."

Nicola's gargling had stopped, and she'd managed to control her breathing. Her body bobbed with each inhalation and exhalation, eyelids flickering open and shut.

"This is our world now," the man continued. "We are the ones tasked with rebuilding his earth and believe me, our work will not begin here. God has chosen the place and that's where we will return."

My shaking hand closed around Nicola's gun. I thought of Eri, her face flushed like the fruits my father once spoke of. How long would she wait before giving up and believing me dead? What form would my story take? Would I always be out there somewhere, struggling to make it back home? A phantom parent haunting the dreams of my child?

One of the lights gave out, plunging the vault into almost darkness and breaking these maddening thoughts. I emerged from the boxes, screaming and firing. He shot my coat sleeve, the bullet passing straight through the foam and knocking my hand away, but I didn't stop until my ammo ran out.

He was splayed on the floor, his legs twisted, a dark pool forming on the ground. I flipped him over, with my boot. I'd hit him a couple of times – once in the arm and the other in the neck. His eyes glistened, and blood oozed from his mouth. Kneeling to get a closer look, I confirmed his youth, younger than me, but like me, he was a child during the fall. Acknowledging this, I placed a regretful hand on his shoulder.

Nicola moaned behind me, and I stood again, collecting the man's rifle, discarded by his side. I poked the barrel into his mouth and fired, the shot ringing around the walls, dislodging ice from the roof.

I tossed the rifle aside and turned to find that Nicola had crawled over to a body. She'd managed to sit up too, her hand still covering her stomach, though it appeared the injury might not be as bad as it looked. She handed me a folded plastic wallet containing a list of codes and numbers.

"Go, collect these," she whispered. "Several of each. I'll take care of these boxes."

In the rear vault, I cradled each box as I lifted them from the shelves. A residual anxiety mixed with an urgency to get Nicola to safety, kept me going. Outside, she was separating pouches into piles, making sure we only took what we needed. Emerging from the third and final vault, breathless and pleased at finishing the task, I found Nicola gone. I called her name, but she didn't reply.

I spotted the blood smears on the concrete heading back out of the main door and into the corridors. Over where Nicola had been working lay a pile of seed packets, behind which was balanced a sheet of cardboard. Stepping closer I saw she'd used her blood to spell 'THESE'. I grabbed them up and added them to my sack. Her sack lay discarded by the boxes, and empty.

Nicola's blood trail finally stopped outside a door at the front of the building. I leant against the door and heard her weeping inside.

"Nicola," I said. "Can I come in?"

She didn't answer so I pushed the door and was jolted by the creak of the ancient hinges.

•

"Everything happened so fast," she said, tears marking her face, her grey hair bunched at the shoulders. "A call came to say the threat level of the remote monitoring station had been raised and the site was being closed down, as was the facility here. Communications were cut off and all the doors were auto-locking."

I started walking toward where she lay, her body hunched and leaning over some object on the floor.

"Wait," she said. "Don't come any nearer, not yet."

I stood by the doorway, holding it open, letting the light from outside cast a shadow over the small space. At the back was a desk with another computer. Shelves bordered the walls with dozens of books which hadn't yet gone to rot. The room smelled, though. A sickening stench trapped here for over a decade, now finally dispersing into the corridor.

"Thankfully none of us were inside a vault at that point," Nicola continued, "so, we ran from the main area, smashing through the access doors until we came to the corridors here, but it was too late. All the rooms were sealed."

"What about the entrance?" I said.

Nicola gave off a frustrated snort and wiped away her tears.

"Serena. My partner. She had gone outside for a smoke and, through complete luck I guess, had leant against the open door rather than stepping outside completely. I screamed at her, 'Where's your fucking key, where's your fucking key?' but of course our keys by that point were voided. The place was sealed, the seeds preserved and safe from human hands."

"Oh God, Nic…" I started to say, but she moved, my chest swelled, and I was in the corridor again, emptying my stomach on the cold stone floor.

•

A tiny skull, a sliver of spinal cord and a rib cage which had cracked from the pressure applied by the strap which held the body in its carrier. Pitch black sockets and what could only be a faint smile. I hoped it was a smile. It must have wailed for days, abandoned and cold, with the silence slowly squeezing out its life.

I sat beside Nicola now, placed an arm around her and used the baby's blanket to cover its remains.

After a while, she started talking again. "I was pregnant when we arrived. I didn't know at the time otherwise we wouldn't have come. And I couldn't go back, because Serena would have had to stay and that would have been unbearable. So, we asked the others stationed here to keep our secret, and I worked right up until my labour and gave birth a week before the shutdown. It was the first time I'd left her alone with Serena. I'd just gone for a walk, to check up on the guys and see how they were doing. Of course, we separated soon after returning home and everything fell apart."

I stayed silent, gripping tightly to her old frame, choking back my own tears.

"My plan was always to die here with her," she continued. "But I found you, and Lasse and Leif and everyone else and I had a purpose. You all gave me a purpose, and joy, and happiness. Yet after it all, here I am."

•

Ada had fallen asleep in my arms. The fire had turned her face bright red, and some drool had formed on her face. I wiped it away with my sleeve and lifted her up. Through the barley fields, I walked back to our home.

Above, the night sky flickered with wisps of green and purple, dancing amongst an infinite sea of stars.

•

Andrew Openshaw is a speculative fiction writer from Newcastle upon Tyne in the UK. Married to Josephine, he is a proud parent to the world's noisiest cats, Maxwell, Molko and Bodhi.

Find out more at www.andrewopenshaw.com

HER JOURNEY
(A LOST SONS STORY)

A.L. BUXTON

Josanne woke as she had gone to sleep, naked. She sat upright, her messy red hair hanging down, covering her breasts. She stretched out, rose and went to the table in the corner of the tent, pouring a goblet of water. She drank it in one and began dressing.

"Awake at this time?" asked Ada. He sat up, his top half bare except for the tattoos, black lines wrapping over his muscled chest. His long black hair was greasy and thick, his beard bushy and his eyes bold.

"The birds chirp," she replied.

He watched her dress, smiling and observing.

"Marry me," he said.

She turned and stared at him before erupting into a man like roar.

He laughed back briefly before pressing. "Come on, why not?"

"You're a fool, Ada. You've known me half a year and only by sight. I am still a stranger to you," she said.

He rose and made for the table. "You do not enjoy me?" he asked. He plucked grapes and chewed on them noisily.

"I enjoy our evenings together, yes, but do not forget my father used to mention marriage all too often. I left him. I will leave you," she said.

Ada choked on a grape and burst out laughing.

"Such a strange woman," he blurted out. He turned and strode towards her, grabbing her hard. "But what a woman."

"And don't you forget it, Ada," she said. She pulled from him, sheathed her blade and fitted her boots as he did the same. "I will gather the pit. Meet me out there presently."

Josanne bailed from the tent and went out into the camp. The children had risen early and were playing with sparring swords whilst a couple of soldiers patrolled or helped the elderly with their tasks. The few warriors that Ada had managed to recruit were dressed in furs as they could not afford armour and their swords were not the sharpest and certainly not castle forged.

"Gather at the pit, everyone. Ada will speak!" shouted Josanne.

The people came to a halt and at once they rushed to the centre of the camp. A long trail of wooden seats surrounded a pit that dipped into the earth.

The camp held a capacity of nearly forty people and Ada was their leader. He was a man who had come from nothing but an abusive childhood and parents who were drunks. When he reached the age of fifteen, he'd abandoned them. He fled the city of Rievaulx and joined a charitable band of helpers, workers and fighters. For twelve years he had stuck with them, he had watched four leaders perish to raiding gang attacks and now he found himself leading. Josanne had joined them six months ago.

"Thank you all for gathering," announced Ada as he came from his tent. He brushed between the seated people and headed for the middle of the pit.

"As you all know, we may have to relocate soon. The torturous gangs are scouting us every day, good men have died whilst scavenging and now I fear for our survival. We laid traps four days ago so this morning, Josanne, Edgar, myself and Cecily will head out and investigate. What we discover will determine our actions. Moira, you will as always provide the rations for the people leaving. The rest of you will have a pack. Be ready to leave. Keep the children within the camp. No venturing today," he announced.

Edgar nodded to Cecily.

"The rations are already prepared, Lord," said Moira, an old woman of nearly seventy.

"No need to call me Lord, Moira. I am but a servant of my people," he said.

She stood and began shifting away from the pit.

"I have added carrots to the stew this morning. Cecily found some yesterday, my Lord," she said as she made for her cooking station.

The people around the pit laughed.

"You heard that, people, go get your carrots. Josanne, Cecily and Edgar, we leave now."

The pit emptied quickly. Cecily, a short man with brown hair and a ginger beard, sheathed his blade and knotted his cloak. Edgar, tall and dark, did the same. They all headed to the border of the forest and waited for Ada as he came bounding through camp.

"Nothing drastic, stay close and stay safe today," said Josanne. "They may be closer than we think."

"How close are we talking?" asked Ada with a certain gaze.

Edgar laughed before Josanne slapped him on his arm.

"Focus!" she demanded.

"It's hard not to with you always reminding me. Focus, she says, boys, focus!" he mocked.

"You will sleep with the pigs tonight, funny man. And Edgar, for laughing, you will take the night watch. Now move out," she said.

Ada couldn't help but smile, Edgar however did not.

•

The four of them travelled through tough terrain, nettle infested bushes and many mounds that grew thick with veins that snatched at the ankles. It took over an hour before they reached the first trap, all tampered with and knotted. Edgar knelt by it and began rummaging.

"What is it?" asked Ada as he signalled to Cecily to watch the perimeter.

"A shoe, a child's shoe," said Edgar as he held it up. It was torn and pitted.

"Do the savages bring children to battle now?" asked Cecily with his back turned to the group.

"This isn't them. This is someone else," said Ada, but he was cut off before he could finish speaking.

A hooded character dropped from the tree above him and held a knife to his throat. Another character, hooded and cloaked, tackled Cecily, beating him briefly before aiming his sword to his face.

A man even larger and taller than Ada pushed Josanne up against the tree. She drew her blade, but her attacker slammed it back in its sheath and stepped back. He pointed an axe at her and smiled through his blond plaited beard.

"Don't harm my people," insisted Ada, his voice croaky from the knife that rested on his jugular. "You're not the people we seek. We have food we can give you for your journey."

"Who are you? Why do you lay these traps?" asked one of the characters as he pulled down his hood. He revealed his rough black bearded face. He had thin slit eyes and long brown hair. He dragged Edgar to his feet and scraped his sword aside with his foot. "Speak quickly."

"My name is Ada. The man you mean to kill is Edgar. That is Cecily and that is my wife, Josanne," said Ada.

"I am not his wife," she groaned.

Her attacker smiled even wider now. "These two men are my brothers and the big one is Doxass. We mean only to pass. But my brother's son stumbled in one of your traps. He nearly lost his leg. He's four," said the man fiercely.

"The traps are defence, not a form of attack," said Josanne.

"Defence against who?" asked the man.

"Raiders, thieves, rapers, gang members, take your pick," said Josanne. "We run a camp barely an hour south of here. It's mostly old people and children but we have some warriors. Anyone is welcome. You can come see for yourself."

"As long as you leave these knives behind," snarled Ada.

The man released Edgar and nodded to his brothers, who each released their targets and approached.

"These pose no threat, brother," said another man, short and young in the face.

"I agree, and I am in need of an ale and some meat," said the other brother, hairier than the others.

"We haven't eaten in days. We have a woman and two children, my brother's family, we can eat with you tonight?" asked the man who seemed to be in command of the group.

" You can," replied Ada, "But like I said, I will be taking your weapons and if I sense at any second that you pose a threat, I will not hesitate."

"Nor I," chanted Josanne.

Doxass laughed hard. He slid his axe onto his back and walked up to Ada, patting him on the back. "Lead the way, funny man, I'm hungry."

•

Everyone again gathered at the pit, seating themselves on the wooden stumps present. They all looked to a group of five men, one woman and two young boys, one four and one twelve. They clustered together, all smelling, all glaring at Moira's pot of stew.

"Thank you all for gathering, I have an announcement," declared Ada. "The traps were untouched and there was no sign of the raider gang. Perhaps they bumped into our new friends, that would for sure scare them off. I would show my gratitude if you could all welcome Doxass, Ornella and their group to the camp. Those are the only two names I know as the others seem rather reluctant on revealing. Maybe some of you can figure it out. Offer them food, aid, set them up a couple of tents and make them welcome. In return, you might be rewarded with some sparring sessions, they can fight, I know that. Their behaviour over the next few days will determine whether their permanent stay is authorised."

"No need for that," said the man who seemed to do all the talking for the group. "We seek only replenishment, although my brothers and friends would be happy to spar with some of your people. But we do not mean to stay."

"The choice is your own," said Josanne before Ada could speak. "But whilst you're here, you will follow the rules and respect our ways."

"Of course," replied Ornella. "Me and my youngest will help with the cleaning and washing. I can cook too, skin a deer if I need to."

"That will be useful, thank you. Go with Moira, she will

keep you. Can't say I've came across many women who can skin a deer," said Ada.

"My wife knows how to survive," interrupted the smallest brother. His hair was shoulder length and his face hairless but dirty.

"I can see that. Now disband, everyone, Moira's stew is ready," said Ada.

The pit once again emptied and everyone disbanded to fill their bowls, all except Josanne. The group took advantage of the quiet and seated themselves around the pit. Ornella, her husband and the boys went off to get set up whilst the four other men sat down.

"Where you from?" asked Josanne, a bowl of stew in her hands.

"West," replied the more brutish brother.

"Whereabouts in the West?" she pressed.

"Just West," snarled Doxass.

"Forgive my brother. He has no manners," said a man who had not yet spoken. He was short with a black beard and very short hair. "My name is Faizer. I want to thank you for taking us in. For weeks we have gone to sleep hungry. It's been a tough road."

"Faizer. So we have three names now, what about you two?" she asked, looking to the other two brothers.

"Not important," said Faizer. "They're good men, that's all you need to know."

"So I'm guessing you're all brothers?" she asked.

"No, Doxass is my brother. We're from Vaughan. We

joined this group more than a year ago. It was just the three of them, Ornella and the boys before that," said Faizer.

"Good men, you say?" said Josanne.

"As good as any other," said Faizer whilst the two brothers glared at Josanne.

"So good men that refuse to share their names? Brothers that live in the forest away from every kind of civilization, experts at camouflage and handy with sword and dagger? Forgive me for speaking out, but they're not exactly the traits of good men," she said.

"We mean no harm on your people. I can see that you're nervous," said the man in command.

"I don't get nervous," she snapped. "You know, I have heard of such a group of your kind. Western brothers, living in the forest. Have you heard of King Artaxes?"

"Heard of him," snapped the brutish brother.

"Hmm, banished his three sons, I heard. Condemned them to a life of quarantine I heard," she said.

"I heard the King was mad," said the main brother. He stood. "Your southern perimeter is weak. I noticed at least two ways of entry for your raider gang should they attack. Me and my brother will hold watch the tonight, the rest of our group will feast with you and sleep. Tomorrow, Faizer and Doxass will man the watch. The morning after we will be gone." He left the pit along with his brother.

"Stew looks good. Best we have had in weeks," said Ornella as she came. She handed Doxass and Faizer a bowl each before sitting next to them. The two boys did the same.

"How old are you?" asked Josanne, her question directed to the smallest boy. He held great resemblance to his father who had just joined with Ada, talking peacefully by Moira's station.

"I'm four. My names Armel. What's your name?" asked the boy.

His mother gave him a certain look.

"Armel, interesting," Josanne said, looking into Faizer's worried gaze. "My name is Josanne. I help around here. You are safe now, little man."

"I'm always safe. My uncles protect me," he replied as he struggled to eat his stew.

"Let me help you," said the other boy. He was tall for twelve, his hair either blond or brown, you could not yet tell, and his skin pale like his father's. His mother patted him on the back with a smile as he helped his brother.

"Thank you for your hospitality, I don't think my husband wants to stay too long, but you have our gratitude," said Ornella.

"I've gathered, and you're welcome," said Josanne. She finished her bowl and placed it on the ground, walking to her tent and bringing back a tray of horns and a casket of ale.

"I like this woman," said Doxass. He had finished his stew almost immediately and now looked with wet lips at the ale. Josanne filled his up first, then handed one to Faizer, one to Ornella and sat back down.

"You forgot me," said the teenage boy, stern.

Josanne looked to his mother for approval to which she nodded without hesitation. Josanne filled him up a horn of ale and sat back down.

"Drink up, little man. Enjoy it whilst you can," said Faizer. He smashed his own horn of ale off the boy's and then ruffled his hair so hard he nearly knocked him off the bench.

"So where will you be heading to next, when you leave?" asked Josanne.

"You ask a lot of questions, don't you?" said Ornella. "Where is it you're from anyway? Your hair is too pretty so you can't have lived here too long. Your skin as well, it looks soft, I can tell that by sitting all the way over here. You're royalty maybe, no not royalty, high born at least. Auridion? No, Brigantium. Is Tobias Ringfold your King?"

"At least I know now who the clever one is," said Josanne. She shrugged and drank away.

"My youngest son is cleverer than most. There are no fools among our Company," said Ornella.

"That man there," Doxass interrupted. "The one with the markings on his body, the big one."

"Ada?" asked Josanne.

"He your man?" he replied with a smile.

She looked back, curious and yet confused. "That matters why?" she asked.

"Because you are a beauty, and I want to know if you have a man?" he asked.

Ornella smacked him on the side.

"That is my cue to leave. I will sing for the men and woman tonight, if Ada allows it. I know you have your rules," said Ornella. She stood and guided her two boys away.

"He is my man, but do not be mistaken, I do not need him to protect me. If you step near me, I will cut you down," threatened Josanne, ignoring Ornella's departure.

"Have no fear with me, I am a gentle beast. My brother calls me that often enough. But curiosity is curiosity. Forgive me, it's been a long road and I intend to sleep until the sun sets and rises again." He stood, helped and himself to another ale and left.

•

Josanne woke the next morning, Ada had already risen and headed out on an expedition. He was still concerned about the threat at hand. The night before he had confided in Josanne; he wanted her to help him persuade their newfound friends to stay. He knew his camp was weak and they needed reinforcing. She had agreed to help fulfil his ambitions, so they drank wine together, spoke of more plans and then lay with one another. The same routine as most nights of late. That's one thing Josanne did not like, routine. She hated not having a purpose, a dream or an ambition to chase. She did not like to stay in the same place for too long.

Josanne shared breakfast with Edgar's wife that

morning, all the time monitoring the new group. She watched the two oldest brothers spar whilst the youngest one helped structure a new style of tent. He showed one of the builders, Mandor, how to extend a small tent using only thick poles, salvaged from the forest. Doxass and Faizer seemed to crop up every now and again from the forest too. When she asked them, they explained that they were checking for weak spots and advised extending the perimeter's watch. Josanne however didn't have the men.

After the sun had hit its highest point, Josanne relieved one of the warriors who manned the northern side of the camp. Ada was taking his time, long overdue and her worry grew. She knew he would return from the northern side, so she supped at a horn of ale and waited. It was close to dark when they returned.

"Edgar," she signalled.

It wasn't until he came fully out of the bush that she realised he was wounded and worse than that, he was alone.

"Josanne, they have him!" spat Edgar, a gash on his arm and multiple bruises on his face.

She darted towards him. "You're bleeding. What happened? Where is Ada? Where is Cecily and the others?"

"Cecily is dead, the others too. Ada was about to take an axe to the neck until I called out his name. Once they realised who he was, they bound his arms and took him. He was too badly wounded to fight back. Three stayed behind to finish me off but I escaped."

"He won't live out the night," said a voice from behind.

Josanne drew her blade, Edgar too. It was the brother who spoke for the group.

"What do you know of it?" she blasted before turning to Edgar. "Ready the men, everyone we have, we must go after them."

"You have to put your camp first," interrupted the brother.

"That is Ada's job. That is why we must get him back," she growled.

"My youngest brother can track. He can do it at night if he has to, and my other brother can fight better than any man I've ever seen. We will go, if Edgar agrees to guide us," he said.

"I will, if Josanne grants me permission," said Edgar.

"I am not your leader. You will make your own choice, Edgar, but I will come along too," she said.

"You cannot, whether you want to lead or not, you have no choice now. You must have your camp packed up and ready to leave. My two friends Doxass and Faizer will stay behind and help you. They can fight if they need to, better than any of your perimeter guards, I promise you," he said.

"Ada needs me. I will come," she attempted to argue.

"You need us if you want him back alive. I request you heed my advice. Those people back at that camp need you. If we fall on this quest, there will be no one left to protect them," he said as he approached her. "I'm sure you've seen war before, no matter how big or small it is, you're an Easterner Ornella tells me. If that is true, then you have experienced conflict. So, you know what happens to the women up there, should we die, and your camp be left unprotected? You know what happens to the children, don't you? Heed my advice, Josanne."

"I will stay with the camp," she said with a struggle.

"Edgar, I will assemble my brothers, you need to be ready to leave in a moment," said the brother.

"I will be ready," he nodded.

"Thank you," muttered Josanne, the brother looked back at her for but a moment before disappearing back up to the camp.

•

Josanne struggled to control the camp. Panic had broken out as soon as she told them of Ada's capture. If it were Ada himself, he would have kept it a secret until the issue had been resolved. He would not want to worry the people, but Josanne was different, she would never lie to anyone, no matter the consequence. She believed the camp to be one, so all information was shared.

It was night, only the torches and the fires at the pit kept the camp alight. Faizer and Doxass managed the warriors that remained, and soon had them all armed and ready, should the fight come to them. The women kept the children safe whilst the men that could not fight packed away the tents and loaded the carriages. Throughout all this Josanne stood, sword in hand, shield at the ready.

"They will come back, won't they?" asked Edgar's young wife. Her name was Dea. Edgar was only twenty and nine himself, but his wife was still a child. Her twentieth name day had only just passed and what known feeling could match young love. She hadn't stopped sobbing since the second he had returned, bleeding from his sword arm. She was blonde, short and thin, with eyes as green as emeralds.

"I'm sure they will," said Josanne, disinterested, her mind elsewhere.

"But these men, these brothers, we don't know them. Edgar has gone with them alone," said Dea.

"They are strangers, yes, but as Faizer say's, they're good men. There is more to them, I know that for sure," said Josanne.

"Who, who's Faizer?" asked Dea, her face ugly for a change as she cried uncontrollably.

"Wipe it from your mind, you have to be strong now." Josanne turned to her. "Edgar is one of the best fighters in this camp. He will prevail. Go help Moira, she is struggling. Let me worry about the rest."

"I will do all I can," she accepted, drying her cheeks. "He loves me too much to leave. He will come back."

Josanne watched her leave and embraced the stab of guilt she felt. For the first time she had lied to someone in this camp. Edgar was a reckless fighter; he barely knew the sword and god forbid was he ever to pick up a bow. Should they engage in combat, his chance of survival would be slim.

A few more hours passed and the camp still ran ragged. The longer it took for them to return, the worse the people behaved. Dea could be heard crying all around whilst Doxass's roar matched it well. Josanne observed him for most of the night. The man who seemed like a barbarian, who took what he wanted, had revealed his true self. He was caring, respectful and extremely organised, like his brother Faizer. He helped the men load the carriages, lifting double the weight that they did whilst speaking funny words into the scared children's ears, their laughter seeming to bring him joy because he laughed twice as loud as he normally did.

Josanne had almost lost herself in the moment of admiring the big man, when a loud crunching coming from the eastern side of the camp brought her back to realisation.

"Swords!" she roared.

A handful of men and even some of the women grabbed weapons and raced towards her. Faizer commanded the soldiers into formation, a tactic that he had taught them all that afternoon. They made a thin line and raised their shields together. Doxass, Josanne and Faizer stood in front of the line, swaying with their weapons at the ready.

"Gideon," Josanne heard Faizer whisper to himself as he lowered his sword and looked before snapping back to the trees. Ada burst out, bleeding from the head, a gashed ear and two missing fingers. The two older brothers dragged him in, whilst the youngest brother followed, covered in blood, not of his own.

"Ada!" Josanne screamed. She raced over and held him as they dropped him down.

"Bastards can fight," he grunted. Josanne laughed and rubbed his hair. "Get me up, get me up!"

"You're wounded. Someone bring water, quick!" shouted Josanne, but Ada had risen. He stood up straight and spoke to the people.

"You can unpack the wagons, we're not going anywhere," he sounded. "Did I not tell you our friends could fight. The gang that has terrorised us for months has been vanquished."

"Vanquished?" asked Josanne as she looked to the three brothers.

Each one of them were barely out of breath. They simply wiped the blood from their swords, knives and daggers without seeking any form of praise. Ornella had tended to them at once, offering her husband water and then his brothers. Josanne respected them now, and a great sense of relief and safety hit her. She found herself in a happy state until the whimpering of Dea dampened everyone's cheering.

"Ada!" she screamed as she came over, almost falling to the ground with each step. "Where is he, Ada? Where is Edgar, where is my love?"

Ada looked down and rested his able hand on her shoulder, but before he could speak the main brother intervened.

"Edgar died, girl, fighting for his leader. He killed many foes. Without his help Ada and my brothers would have died," he said.

Her face crumpled with each word before she fell to her knees sobbing, her heart, broken. "Dead?" she asked.

The brother dropped to his knees with her, whilst the people observed.

"I took this from his body," he said as he pulled out a necklace with a sharp talisman confined in a ruby jewel. "He spoke of you all the way there, told me that if he were to fall I should bring you this. It's a token of his love, Dea."

"You made him go, you mad, mad man! You killed him." She fell hysteric.

Ada approached and lifted her up.

"Dry your eyes, girl, these men are not to blame. Our camp's survival is because of them. Tonight, we drink ale in Edgar's memory for our home is saved," said Ada.

Everyone cheered but Dea. Her mother and sister came from the crowd and took her off to grieve in their own way.

"Come with me, Ada, we must get you cleaned up," said Josanne. She took him into the tent and, dabbing a cloth in a bowl of water, she began to rub the dry blood from his wounds. "Tell me what it was like. What they did to you?"

"They tortured me for a day for information on the camp's whereabouts, then planned to execute me and bring my head back here. They would have taken our women for their own and enslaved the children. Our new friends killed them all before they could. The youngest brother killed a dozen before I knew what was happening.

Throwing knives… I've never seen them thrown like that," he explained as if amazed.

"And Edgar?" she asked.

Ada frowned. "He died with his sword still dry," he said.

"So, the travellers lied to Dea," she said.

"They saved her the pain of her knowing he died a coward; they gave him a warrior's death even though he had not earned it. Yet, he came to rescue me, so he has my respect. But when the fighting began, he ran, he took a shaft through the spine," said Ada.

Josanne looked at it a different way now, and a smile invaded her face.

•

The celebration raged right into the night. Ada had passed out after many slurred speeches in honour of the group that saved him. Toasts were made to Edgar, Cecily and the other men that died, and a small feast prepared, then devoured. Most people had now taken to their tents. Women and their men could be heard laying with one another whilst heavy snoring could be heard elsewhere. The laughter of Doxass and his brother echoed still as they wrestled drunk in the mud. Josanne hadn't drunk much. She had gone to see Dea for a while before sitting quietly around the pit. She now found herself alone with the main brother of the Company. He sipped lightly on an ale, never seeming to get drunk.

"Thank you for today," she said as they sat opposite each other around the pit.

"It was the right thing to do. He's brutish, but he's good, I could tell that from the beginning," he replied.

"He loves you already, all of you," she said. "He will expect you to stay now," she added.

His eyes flicked up at her. "We mean to move on. We will help reorganise for a while, but we will go," he said.

"I know, and I will be coming with you," she said, taking him by surprise.

"Somehow I feel like a life on the road is not for you, a noble's daughter," he said.

"I've been on the road for years. I've fought, I've been beaten, raped, kidnapped and cut. I've experienced it all. I could return East tomorrow should I desire it. I could wear the finest gowns and gather at King Tobias's court if I wanted. But I choose my own path. I choose you, Gideon Destain," she announced.

He choked on his swig, spitting the ale onto the floor.

"What did you call me?" he asked.

"I am no fool, I put together the pieces. You're the heir to the Meridium throne, those are your brothers, King Artaxes's sons," she said.

Before he could speak, she cut him off. "Worry not, your secret will never leave my lips. I know why you keep it and I intend to help you on your journey. I am ready to leave as soon as you are." She stood and left his company.

"I'm sorry for what you have experienced," he said, making her stop. "We have experienced the same, and I would be honoured for you to join us."

•

Anthony Buxton became an author at the age of 22, writing his series The Lost Sons of the West. He currently has two books in the series released and four short stories, in volumes of Harvey Duckman Presents. Anthony also runs a new, modern blog where he shares stories of his personal life as well as in depth information about his book series and his plans for the future.

Check out his blog at
anthonybuxtondotblog.wordpress.com

THE LONELY OAK
(A TALE OF THE WOODS)

JOSEPH CARRABIS

Once upon a time, in a land almost too far away, there lived a tall, glorious oak. It wasn't odd at all that a tall, glorious oak should live in this land for this land was a Woods. But this Woods wasn't like any woods or forests you've ever seen before. Here the animals talked and flowers flew and trees moved wherever they needed. This was a magical Woods, unlike most others.

You understand, don't you? It's magic, after all.

This tall oak watched all around her. She wasn't old as oaks go in years, but she was a wise oak just the same. She had been an oak all her life. And all her life she had seen things in the Woods. Good things and bad things, sad things and glad things. And everything she saw she held deep inside, deep where the blood of trees flows from the roots in the ground to the high crown of leaves that brace the sky.

One of the things she'd seen often was the love of others for the trees around her. This made her glad. 'Someday,' she thought, 'someone will come and love me.'

She waited for some time, through many seasons in fact. But no one came. Many came through the Woods where she lived and spread her leaves, but all that came seemed to prefer the shade of other trees. The tall oak watched this and wondered, 'Is there something wrong with my leaves? Or my bark? Perhaps I don't shade the world as I might?'

None of this was true of course. The oak's leaves were among the most beautiful in the Woods. Her bark was clean and smooth and ran straighter than many other trees. Her shade was a peaceful relief to the small creatures that sought shelter under her.

But all this wonderful oak saw was the scores of others resting under other trees. 'Perhaps I'm too tall a tree?'

And so, despite the fact that she was a beautiful oak, she let her boughs drop to her sides and twisted her trunk slightly, trying to make herself smaller in the Woods.

It didn't work of course. Few such things ever do. There are few creatures that can hide what they are from those with eyes to see, and those with eyes to see have much magic about them. This oak had a magic, too, but not one that would allow her to hide what she was from those who wished to see.

And, of course, trying to be what you are not is not what the Woods wish. Far away in the Woods, far deeper in the Woods than the oak had ever thought to go, a messenger was sent, a small butterfly dispatched to tell the oak her slumping and slouching would not make her loved.

The butterfly flew all the miles to where the tall oak stood and looked at her. But what the butterfly saw was not what she expected to see. There was an oak, a glorious tree, one that should be tall and proud in the Woods, huddled over and letting her leaves touch the ground.

The butterfly flew up to the tree and said, "Excuse me, but isn't there an oak close by?"

The oak shook a little at this. Should she stay crouched and huddled, trying to be some other tree, or quickly right herself and show she was an oak? "No, just me. There was an oak here, but now she's gone."

"And what are you, fair tree?"

"I am a supple, wind-swept willow, graceful and growing here in the Woods."

The butterfly flew around the oak once, twice, then once again. "You're not a willow. I think," she said, eying the oak's leaves and roots, "I think you are a beautiful tree. But not a willow."

"What kind of tree am I, then?" the oak asked, fearful yet happy that someone found her attractive in the Woods. "What kind of tree do you see?"

The butterfly smiled at her. "Willows," she said, "cannot stand the wind. Perhaps the wind will show me what kind of tree you are." The butterfly flew around the oak again. Then another time, only faster. Then faster and faster and faster until the butterfly became a blur to the oak's eyes. As she flew, a whirlwind came up from her wings, for this butterfly carried some magic of the Woods inside herself, and the magic of this butterfly was to make others glad.

The butterfly flew until great winds pulled at the tree's bent form. The winds pulled her boughs from the ground and lifted her branches high into the air. Her trunk once again grew straight and tall and soared into the sky.

And all the while the winds pulled at her, the oak heard the butterfly's voice calling, "Most beautiful of trees, most glorious of oaks. Raise yourself up. You are the most wonderful of your kind in the Woods." Faster and faster the winds swept around her. Taller and taller they forced her to stand. In between the butterfly's words the oak heard the butterfly's laughter, laughter that did not mock but glowed with a warming fire only found deep, deep in the Woods. The butterfly flew faster and her words grew stronger and her laughter louder until they swam in the air around Sister Oak, making her glad she was an oak in the Woods.

Suddenly, and although she couldn't see it, fire burst through the butterfly's wings. The fires ripped through Sister Oak as they burned, forcing the things she kept deep to come up and move through her. A strange thing happened then. Everything she carried so deep, every hurt and pain and joy and love she had, she suddenly realised were what made her the most beautiful of trees in the Woods.

All creatures have hurts and pains. It is what we do with those hurts and pains that make us what we are in the Woods. Sister Oak realised that hiding them made her wish she wasn't an oak tree at all. Sharing them made her

Sister Oak, an oak more wonderful than most creatures' eyes could see.

The butterfly's whirlwind continued for a time. Slowly the winds grew less, but Sister Oak stood tall and firm. When the wind completely stopped, Sister Oak saw the butterfly was gone. But she heard a singing. A soft, sweet singing. High in her branches, a small white bird sang. Beneath her, where roots buried themselves in the ground, creatures relaxed in her shade.

•

Joseph Carrabis is boring and dull (his words, not ours).

Also by Jospeh Carrabis

The Augmented Man
Empty Sky
Tales Told 'Round Celestial Campfires

Find out more at his blog and on social media:
https://josephcarrabis.com

HOW TO KILL AN UNKILLABLE THING

AIDAN CAIRNIE

Every choice you make has an impact. Every decision grows another branch of the tree. In this way, there are millions of realities, some with the slightest of differences, others with unrecognisable qualities. For example, in one such reality you will have never have read these sentences.

This brings us to Victorian London. Not the Victorian London you've heard about, but a variant that was part of the industrial era that never ceased. Through the labyrinth of buildings and towers and roads, every inch was powered by steam and clockwork. The River Thames was churned up by the colossal wheels lining its banks in dozens, powering the industrialised fortress of brick and steam. Zeppelins soared in the skies above, rising from blimp ports in the centre of the city, overshadowing those below, as if these airships were brushes painting the landscape below a shade of dark grey. These blimps were joined by the plumes of steam and smoke in the orange shimmer of the evening sun.

In one of these many winding streets, bordered with

markets and shadows of the towering walls of the estate was an office. A detective's office. And with his back to the window, Lee Grivets. He was a slim man, with outstretched fingers slithering over the files on his desk. He had a gruff expression supported by his grey eyebrows and sideburns, and in one look you could tell he was a serious man indeed. Grivets was attired in a navy-blue unbuttoned trench coat, with a golden badge that gleamed proudly on his breast. To accompany this, a fedora of equal colour was perched on his head. Grivets' piercing hazel eyes had an unwavering determination towards the paperwork in front of him.

The case files laid upon his desk in a countless quantity all addressed the same issue. He scrambled through the pile to find the bottom folder, labelled 'Dr Hector Tirrin'. Looking through it, all the memories flooded back to Grivets, from a year or so before…

•

When Lee Grivets acquired the news that two people had practically vanished, he wasn't surprised, or too worried. Whoever was in charge of the case would solve it in about a week at maximum, due to the sheer rush and clumsiness of a criminal running off with two bodies at once. There was sure to be a trail of breadcrumbs.

Then, two days later, Grivets got a hold of a telegram explaining a body had been found and someone of higher expertise was needed for the investigation. It got his attention. Especially when the letter described the corpse.

A horse and carriage galloped and rolled down beside the alley, where a wannabe detective met Grivets stepping out of the cart before it set off again. The special investigations operative was astonished to see that the newbies weren't throwing up or in shock or crying. After all, even Grivets' younger self couldn't bear to see a corpse in such a state. Not now of course. You get used to the atrocities of criminal making.

Strolling down the closed off alley, a slumped figure finally came into view in the shadows.

"Who has this been identified as? Dr Tirrin or Mr Gibbon?" Detective Grivets enquired. His voice was gruff, but still had a hint of cockney in there.

"We don't know at this current point in time, sir..." the rookie answered.

"You have the pictures. Even if they're in black and white, you should be able to tell from the body," Grivets lectured with a snarl in his voice, leaning towards the corpse.

Then all the pieces from the last few minutes, in as little quantity as they were, came together. Why no one was wavered or off put by this murder. Why they couldn't identify the body. Why a special investigations detective was called in for a petty two-part murder.

The victim was scorched all over, left as black as coal. They had no hair, and rags almost welded to their skin. Any way in which the murdered could have died, any gash, scar or wound was obscured by soot and ash. The eyes were missing, presumably from the combustion, and the fingers were curled as the muscles had tensed in the victim's cellular rot.

"Search London for a second body!" Grivets ordered, suddenly on edge. Whoever did this was more cunning than at first seemed.

"Where in London?" The rookie wanted clarification. "The killers had around thirty-six hours since the abduction, murder, and burning of these people. They could be anywhere from here to the outskirts of this city."

Hours after, police were dispatched across the city, looking for a needle in a haystack. A bloody needle in an industrialised haystack. It had an inevitable outcome. No one found anything. No body, no leads, nothing.

•

That stayed the same for a year or so, with little development apart from a growing number of cases from the same origin. The only decent lead was from the next abduction after the first. A witness saw a man with a cat's eye hurrying to the scene. It sounded ridiculous to think that whoever this was shared a right eye with a cat, but at this point Grivets would take any evidence possible. Yet there was a correlation between sightings of those who vanished to this obscured criminal. They all were around the same area, orbiting a certain point. It sounded as if it was effortless to pinpoint the scoundrel with this theory.

Yet no solution is ever obvious if you've never learnt how to solve the problem. Lee Grivets would've given up this case long ago if it wasn't for the intrigue and frequency of these crimes.

He splayed his hands against the desk and pulled himself up from his chair. He was going to check the main area of disappearances and deaths based on the map on his wall, red crosses marking every confirmed case of this killer. Soon Detective Grivets found himself perched on the steps of his office as a carriage stopped in front of him. Grivets pulled himself into the seat inside the jet-black cart, and the horseman spurred on his steed to its next destination.

The night sky began to drown out the entrancing light of the setting sun. Curfew. The markets passed by became empty, the bustle and hustle of the streets became silenced by its emptiness. Then, what happened next even the detective couldn't foresee...

The sudden cry of a horse caught Grivets by surprise. He rushed to the carriage door as the vehicle shuddered to a stop and dived out to see a trail of blood heading into an alley.

"Damn! They were here!"

He turned to the horseman's perch jutting out from the bulk of the passengers' compartment. There the poor man lay groaning, a wound in his side. However, it seemed it was not the wound bothering the man, but some kind of unforgiving ill. Detective Grivets, still vigilant, turned to the reins, disconnected from the horse, for there was no steed. Someone had taken it; the road of crimson liquid was presumably the pitied creature's.

Grivets had kept an eye on every missing animal, cat posters, zoo escapes, missing stallions since the 'man with a cat's eye' was spotted. From that he could infer that whoever was behind all this wanted to murder more than just humans.

At that moment he could have easily followed the trail and caught up with the attacker, but there was something more important.

He turned to the injured coachman.

"Hang on in there. You're now under witness protection…"

•

The police station was empty. Grivets didn't like to be here. He much preferred the quiet and professionalism of his secluded office. That was why he was glad that he came during curfew, while the coppers were on high alert for criminals lurking in the dark. It also helped it was one in the morning.

The room Lee Grivets sat in was empty apart from a table and a few chairs. Devoid of distractions so it could be straight to the point. The interrogation room. The detective remembered when interrogation wasn't a thing, and people would be given the death penalty just for the pettiest of offences. But it was the 21st century, for goodness sake. Now capital punishment was only for murder and treason, so people retained the right to be innocent in court. He supposed this was better, as he himself had found evidence to prove innocence after the person in question had been executed. It could really break you at times.

The door slid open and Sergeant Anne Bentley, head of this station strolled in. She was a brunette with a serious face and green eyes which could almost hypnotise a person, and not in the way you would think. They contained an extreme intimidation that seemed to slice up those of inferior rank. That's why she was glad to see someone of the same importance joining herself in the interrogation. Someone whose lip wouldn't quiver with one look and treat her as a superior, which she was and it was handy for work, but wasn't good for conversation at lunch break.

"'Ello Grivets," Bentley greeted while sitting down, her cockney accent on front line display in her voice. "Been a while."

"That it has," Grivets replied.

"Well, we've treated the witness for the wound he has, so he should be fine for this."

"I doubt that included any internal wounds... The injuries of the mind..."

The door slid open and a constable with an iconic towering hat escorted the coachman in, before leaving to monitor the conversation through a slit in the wall.

The horseman had grey hair snaking down into a small beard on his chin. He was attired with a dark suit with frilly sleeves, and his face, that disturbed face. A permanent state of panic, shaking and quivering, his eyes darted about the room and he twisted and turned to see if anything lurked behind him. He was as pale as snow and still looked deadly ill.

"So, we'd like to know who attacked you," Bentley enquired.

At the other end of the table the carter muttered. "Not who. Not who. N-Not who…"

"Okay then, 'what' was it?" Grivets pressed forward.

"Yes, yes, yes! It is a what! A thing…" the horseman rambled,

"What does this 'thing' look like?"

The man furrowed his brow and looked like he was having an extreme headache. He whacked his head against the table and tears streamed down his cheeks.

"Calm down," Sergeant Bentley advised.

"Three, it had three, its eye, that eye! Like a slit! It had these scales and a mouth with all those teeth, and it bit me! Oh, it bit me… It, it felt like… coursing through my veins… It hurts!" The mad coachman screeched.

Grivets and Bentley stood up, sensing something was wrong. Then the man threw up onto the floor, as well as coughing up blood. He tried to stand, but he stumbled back, knocking the chair he once was seated upon to the side of the room. The slider in the wall closed, and the constable rushed in to help. By then the mentally scarred horseman was slumped on the floor, devoid of all and any life.

The three stood around the corpse, two in shock. The one who wasn't was Grivets, whose stare was of cold malice.

"He was poisoned. Must have been a rusty knife or drugged blade which wounded him…" Grivets informed.

"Let's finally lock this killer up." Bentley brimmed with determination against whoever had reduced this man to a corpse.

•

It was the morning a few hours later. Lee Grivets and Anne Bentley meandered through the site of the murders. They both remained ever vigilant, trying to find what made this area a prominent site for 'the murders of the cadavers'.

There dwelled a large group of people huddled around a contraption located in the square. That was when Lee Grivets saw it. That was when Lee Grivets solved it.

"The water pumps," the detective mentioned obscurely.

"What?" a confused Bentley enquired.

"Everyone goes to the water pumps," Grivets clarified. "An ideal serial killing plan is to congregate around a point many people go to, then pick off a lone victim leaving at curfew. They rush home, with such haste they don't notice that horror in the shadows…"

"Now we know where these killings are centred around we can be prepared for the next strike. Top work detective!" Bentley congratulated.

"Then we prepare. We need undercover police spanning

the area. Armed undercover police. One gunshot and we can all head to the officer who fired it for back up. I'm not going to lie, one of your constables may die. Heck! Even I might. But we need to stop this killer before any more fall victim to them."

•

It was night. There were about four on the lookout, no excessive amount to arouse suspicions. Grivets, Bentley and the two others were scattered around the neighbourhood. No sign of anyone.

Detective Grivets hastily walked through the street. They had all spread out from the pump to recreate how people would act at curfew. They needed to draw this thing out. A shadow moved out the corner of his eye. He usually at this point would have turned around and fired his gun, but it was too early. They needed to think he hadn't noticed. He turned into a backstreet. Grivets could practically imagine that the killer was brimming with joy that their next victim walked into a secluded alley. In fact this 'next victim' was leading them to a dead end. Not just to a dead end in their path, but a dead end in their life too...

Lee Grivets halted at the brick blockade ahead of him. He heard fast paced steps as soon as he stopped. He turned and raised a gun from his coat, taking the attacker by surprise. They wore a bowler hat and ragged clothes. Their face obscured by a scarf; all Lee could see was a luminous green eye with a huge pupil. '*So it was a cat's eye after all,*' Lee thought, ready end this.

The killer positioned himself, ready to dive to the side after staring down the barrel of Grivets' six shot revolver but was too late. A miniscule spear of lead drilled into their chest while they leaned to the right in an attempt to avoid the breath of the gun. However this did not deter them, and they instead ran a fleet-footed charge past Grivets and climbed up the wall behind at inconceivable speed.

"What in the name of...?" Grivets cursed, his fingers curling in the slots between the bricks. His muscles screamed as he levered himself up a bit and dug his shoes into the wall. He repeated this over and over, his limbs ready to be ripped out of their sockets. He rolled onto the rooftops in the end and caught a glimpse of the attacker a few metres away.

Despite the painful throb in his arms and legs, the adrenaline coursing throughout his body kept him in pursuit. The roof tiles slid underneath his steps, shattering when they fell on the street below. The criminal jumped over the gap between houses, and Grivets, tailing them, leapt to follow. His fingers hooked on the edge of the roof as he hauled himself up to follow. The next jump was at an abandoned mill. A factory too high for this offender to jump. A dead end for sure this time.

Grivets pulled out his pistol and fired a round of bullets. Two made their way into the target's left leg, whilst one slammed into their shoulder. In theory, this should have sent them spinning, but they didn't seem to limp. They didn't even seem to flinch as three off-trajectory lead rounds flashed by.

The mill grew nearer. At this point Grivets realised that there was one of the factory's windows in the attacker's line of sight. The others would be following the sound of gunshot, so in the inevitable case that the window ended up broken and the two ended up in the cotton mill, Grivets would have to keep this killer inside until backup arrived on the scene. So yeah, he didn't fancy his odds.

Then the fleeing attacker dived through the pane of glass. An explosion of shards became suspended in air for a moment as a pursuing Grivets leapt to follow. The two landed on a glass-covered floor amongst machinery. The whirr of zeppelins could be heard from the blimp port next door, and the black of night drained through the remaining windows.

Grivets knew what the result would be but fired a shot into the killer's chest anyway. The figure flinched from the impact, but otherwise it appeared to have no effect.

"No human can withstand five bullets without bleeding or reacting, so I'm beginning to believe that man you poisoned. What are you?" Grivets asked, loading another round in his gun.

"It wasn't poison..." the figure hissed, pulling off their scarf. "It was venom."

Then the ragged black overcoat slid off them.

It was a horror to see. It had pale green scales all over it. One of its eyes bulged from its socket, the pupil expanding and contracting to adjust to the light. The other eye was human, the jade iris darting about as if it was trying to escape. You'd expect this thing to be in fantasy, wearing battle armour, not a dirty white shirt and murky black trousers. Something began to fold out from a rip in the top, resembling a limb. Three. That's what the mad horseman had said. Three. Three arms. The creature was lined with stitched markings, like it had been sewn together. It had been sewn together. It reeked a rotting stench, every part of it decomposing. Then it smiled. Every one of its crooked teeth were not quite the same, as if each and every one had come from a separate mouth.

"Dr Hector Tirrin, at your humble service." The creature bowed courtly as if this was some kind of game.

"So, one of the first two victims was the killer. Explains why we could never find the other body. I should be kicking myself right now. But that leaves the question. By the looks of it there isn't much of your original body left... Why did you do this to yourself, Hector, if you are Hector anymore?" Grivets pressed.

"Well that, I think, is obvious. But that must be just me. Only because you're going to be found dead in the morning, I'll humour you with this. I wish to become the perfect being, the combined strengths of every species without any weaknesses. I'm far from that goal but I'm near enough to kill you without much effort. At the moment, I'm unkillable. I'm the unkillable species!"

The scaled creature burst into delusional laughter, craving to end Lee Grivets right there and then.

"So you burned the bodies to conceal the parts you took…" Grivets paused, knowing he had to get the first attack.

He charged, grasping his gun by the barrel. As soon as he was in range, the butt of the pistol slammed into Dr Tirrin's forehead before he could react. The thing stumbled back, finding the nozzle of a revolver hovering in front of its bloated eye as it fell. One shot would penetrate the brain. The scene felt as if it was slowing down in the heat of the moment.

"I refuse to believe you're unkillable," Grivets muttered to the future corpse.

Then it all sped up. The third arm grasped Grivets' shirt, pulling him down to the floor with Hector. The pistol drifted out of position, and the bullet made its path through the machinery instead. The two grappled on the ground, Tirrin gradually rising, clutching the detective. Then the creature's arm suddenly whipped, sending Grivets through the air and into the wall.

"It was fun, I'll give you that, but I need to go. Busy schedule, hope you understand," Hector Tirrin cackled, hobbling to the steel double door of the mill.

The gate swung open with reluctance and rust, revealing a view of the blimp port next door. Grivets knew what Doctor Tirrin would do. Hijack a blimp and leave to the next location of his killing spree. All this to fuel his own evolving form. Grivets pulled himself up. He could hear Bentley and the other officers pounding on the door behind to get in. He kept limping to the blimp he saw that monstrosity enter. He hopped in as the gears cranked, and the ramp was levered up to close the entrance. The corridor was lined with seats against the walls, all empty. Grivets pushed himself to the control room.

Inside was a huge clockwork contraption, filled with gears and weights and pistons. The globe clock. Every hand indicated the destination and near blimp ports as well as other blimps. It had taken decades just to make the blueprint of it. And amongst it all stood Dr Hector Tirrin. The blimp rose. The hybrid creature turned towards the persistent special investigator.

It didn't even remark on anything. He'd got on its nerves now. Grivets knew what he had to do. This thing really was unkillable, and Grivets had accepted that. He raised his revolver and aimed it into the gears. *He had two shots left*. The thunder of a gunshot rung about the room as mangled lead appeared in the globe clock. The entire system cranked to a stop. At this point they were high in the air, and the zeppelin began to dip.

"We're crashing you idiot!" the creature screamed preparing to launch himself.

Hector, enraged flew across the compartment, narrowly missing Grivets, who ran to the side door. His shirt was in rags after the creature's claws scraped past him. Then he pulled the lever at the exit. As soon as it fell open, air seemed to rush out. Then Tirrin pounced from behind, pinning Grivets just at the edge of the door frame. The two grappled on the floor for a while, the claws of one of Dr Tirrin's hands slowly edged towards Grivets, whose grasp struggled to keep the sickle of a fingernail up. Grivets sent a knuckle into the doctor's cheek, who then flinched and raised his arms for a second. A second for Grivets to yank out his revolver. He then raised his gun up past Hector and to the balloon above. His finger tensed on the trigger, but he hesitated. *What if there was another way to kill this?* A claw pierced Grivets' neck and he coughed up blood. *No. It was too late for him. He had to continue walking on the path he had made for himself.* His heart throbbed, trying to send blood to his head, but a recently opened hole in his neck prevented this. But he didn't gasp for air nor feel the pain. Not for the adrenaline and impact of the decision he was going to make. The decision he had to make. The barrel of the gun lined up with the balloon. He tried to manage some last words, regrets maybe, but all he could manage was a gurgle of blood. His arm began to numb, but he would not let it succumb to the release of death. His finger tensed, as much as it could on the trigger, as his eyelids drew to a close...

So, you want to know how to kill an unkillable thing? You don't. You blow it out of its damned existence.

Aidan Cairnie began writing books at almost thirteen years old, but before that he read a lot, as evident when he managed to get in trouble on more than one occasion for it. He is also part of a book club with other budding authors. Aidan and another member, Zack Willis, are working on a collaboratation and writing a series of books together.

Aidan is also confused on why he is writing about himself in third person.

THE PERFECT HAM SANDWICH

LIZ TUCKWELL

Agent Foster tossed the transchronograph onto Theobald Willis' desk. It landed with a clang. Shocked, Theobald picked it up and checked for damage. The transchronographs were far too valuable to be treated in this way, but that was agents all over. Careless, especially Foster.

"It's broken," Agent Foster said. "Fix it, will you?" An order, not a request.

"What's wrong with it? Is it the chameleon field or the universal translator?"

"Overheating. Takes longer than usual to activate. You're the boffin, you find out. But I need it back pronto."

With that, the tall, broad-shouldered man strode from the office. Theobald narrowed his eyes with dislike. Of all the agents, Foster was his least favourite. He was tempted to put it to the bottom of his to do list, but Foster was the golden boy of the agency. Theobald seemed to be the only one who didn't worship him. He knew this might have something to do with the fact that Foster was young, slim, and good looking while Theobald was balding, fat and nothing to look at.

Theobald changed a couple of chips and oiled the clockwork mechanisms. Then his stomach growled, telling him it was time for food. He'd only had a bowl of dry-as-dust healthy muesli with bog awful soya milk for breakfast. Rabbit droppings would probably have had more flavour. But lucky rabbits weren't being monitored for their food intake and weighed weekly.

He glanced at the clock, only eleven o'clock, too early for lunch. But he had his secret stash of biscuits and cookies. Theobald hurried to his locker and pulled out a few packets, grateful no other technicians worked in the lab that morning. He noted the dwindling mound with concern. It was getting harder and harder to buy them. Then he concentrated on the immediate problem. A Jammy Dodger or a Milk Chocolate Digestive?

He selected a Jammy Dodger, tempted to take two but knowing he had to ration himself. The rules forbade eating or drinking in the lab. Theobald enjoyed sipping his mug of tea and the delicious jam of his biscuit. Unfortunately, he sprayed a few crumbs over the transchronograph but he tipped the device upside down to make sure he'd got rid of them.

Theobald fiddled more with the transchronograph until lunchtime. The Jammy Dodger hadn't done much to satisfy him. He was hungry but unenthusiastic about lunch options since the government had bowed to the large vegetarian contingent and slapped a tax on meat and meat products that put them well beyond the pay packet of normal people. He glowered as he thought about the agents, lucky bastards who could slip across to any alternative timeline they liked and gorge themselves.

The vision of a ham sandwich came to him, all thick-cut buttered bread and thick sliced ham, with yellow mustard oozing out of the edges. He could practically smell the mustard and the fresh white loaf. He salivated and licked his lips. Then he looked at the transchronograph with its green light blinking. It needed testing. If he used it to go to a timeline where ham sandwiches were easily available, well, he was only testing the equipment as per protocol.

He slipped the transchronograph onto his wrist; it resembled a large, bulky sports watch. He programmed it, estimating a timeline far enough away for the vegetarian movement not to hold sway, but close enough that a certain cafe nearby that used to sell ham sandwiches should still exist. Then he pressed the gold screw on the side.

Theobald had his doubts even before he went inside the place. He remembered it as 'Joe's Café' but the sign outside had been amateurishly altered with black paint to say, 'All American Deli'. Still, it was worth a try.

"What I want is a ham sandwich," said Theobald in the crowded deli.

"Honey oat, whole meal, rye, mixed grain, flatbread, Italian herb and cheese, wafer thin ham, low fat ham, cold cut combo, pickles, lettuce, tomato, onion, sweetcorn, green pepper, cucumber?" The efficient young man in a sparkling white tee shirt, behind the counter asked the question without taking a breath. The holes in his ears were nearly closed up.

"Crusty white bread and I think thick cut ham, preferably Wiltshire but it's not essential, oh and English mustard," Theobald said.

"We can't do that."

"Why not?"

"It's not patriotic."

The deli assistant's gaze flicked behind Theobald who turned to see the posters on the wall, proclaiming in red and blue letters – THANK YOU UNCLE SAM FOR SAVING US and UK GOOD, USA BETTER.

Theobald snorted. "Ridiculous."

A hush fell. The customers stared at Theobald and inched away from him. The young man leaned forward. "Listen, grandpa, have you been drinking? Do yourself a favour and pick something else."

"No," said Theobald in a huff and left the shop.

The transchronograph was definitely playing up. Theobald checked his instructions and the settings and tried again.

He didn't notice the two men in dark suits, sunglasses, with an earphone in one ear, who had followed him out of the deli.

They trailed him to a narrow alley. The first man nodded to the other, to hurry around to the other end. He saw the undesirable fiddling with a large watch and then, to his amazement, the undesirable melted into the air.

The other man hurried along from the other side of the alley.

"What the hell? Where'd he go?"

The first man frowned. "Don't blaspheme." Then, "I have no idea." He wasn't about to admit what he had seen and end up an undesirable himself.

Theobald emerged from the alley and went back to Joe's Cafe. Except it was now called 'Blondi'. The entire interior gleamed and sparkled from the glass display cases to the pine tables and chairs.

"What do you want?" the woman with aggressively blonde highlights asked, wiping the spotless counter down with a cloth.

Theobald repeated his request.

The woman stared at him. "Wiltshire ham? We don't have that. Only Black Forest ham or Westphalian ham, the best in the world. And we only do open sandwiches with tomatoes, pickles or cucumbers. No exceptions." She pointed to the board on the wall, then folded her arms.

Theobald sighed. As he turned to go, he noticed the framed photographs on the walls. The first showed a man with dark hair and a toothbrush moustache. *'Our Beloved First Fuhrer'*, the caption read. The next was a fat man with *'Our Beloved Second Fuhrer'*, and so on. He shivered and rushed out of the cafe, making for the alley.

The transchronograph was not working properly. He checked the settings and tried again.

"What would you like, monsieur?" asked a large man with an equally large moustache behind the counter of the cafe. The French Tricolour hung on the wall. There was a profusion of pastries in the display cases.

"What I want is a ham sandwich," Theobald said.

The large man frowned. "Monsieur would like a Croque Monsieur?"

"That's ham and cheese, isn't it? No, I just want a plain ham sandwich."

"We do not have ham sandwiches," the large man declared. "We have Croque Monsieurs or Croque Madams."

"Which are?"

"Croque Monsieur with an oeuf on top."

Theobald shuddered. "Egg? No, thanks, I want a ham sandwich."

"But that is impossible. We do not serve those. Our Croque Monsieurs are excellent. Even the valet to his Imperial Majesty, Napoleon the Seventh, comes here to our humble establishment, for his Croque Monsieurs when he is in England."

"I don't care if Old Harry comes here for one, I don't want one," Theobald said. "Good day."

He left the shop mumbling to himself, "Don't do ham sandwiches, what kind of lunatic asylum is this?" and bumped into a policeman with a bushy moustache and splendid golden epaulettes on his broad shoulders. The policeman growled as he pushed past.

"Apologise!"

Theobald looked back. "Are you talking to me?"

"Indeed I am, you cretin."

"That's rich, coming from a moron in fancy dress."

The man spluttered and lunged forward, grabbing hold of Theobald's arm. "Insulting the Prefect of the Department of Paris."

Alarmed, Theobald tried to shake the man's arm off.

"And now resisting arrest," the man crowed.

This couldn't be happening. Agency staff had to blend in when they went to another timeline, not draw attention to themselves. And suppose they took the transchronograph off him? Frantic, Theobald turned a dial, no easy matter one-handed then jabbed the gold screw.

Phew! He was out in the open, but there was nobody around to witness his arrival. This time the sign read, 'Cleo's Wine Shop'. Not promising, but Theobald was too stubborn not to try. This time, a woman stood behind the counter in a long dress with a translucent veil over her hair.

"What can I get you?" Her voice was low and sultry.

"A plain ham sandwich," Theobald answered without a great deal of hope in his voice.

She frowned. "We can do you a plate of ham and olives and some slices of bread. What's a sandwich?" She turned her head and called, "Lucius, ever heard of a ham sandwich?"

A tall thin man, in a blue tee shirt with a picture of a toga on the front, appeared through a doorway.

"No," he said. "What is it, something new from Nova Roma?"

"Do you have butter?" Theobald asked. He was willing to make the sandwich himself. Never let it be said that he wasn't flexible.

"Butter?" The woman stared. "That's for burns, not bread."

"Never mind," said Theobald. His shoulders drooped. He left the shop.

He would have one more try, he promised himself, in the grimy alley. Theobald fiddled with the settings and pushed the gold screw once again.

A pub with a sign, 'The Old Bull and Bush' beckoned him inside.

The pub was everything an English pub should be, dimly lit, comfortable chairs, a TV switched to mute, and customers talking in low voices as they drank. Everyone looked a little pasty to him but it was probably the light.

The pretty barmaid had greeted him with a friendly smile that displayed her gleaming white teeth. Her hands were surprisingly cold when she passed him the pint.

"I haven't seen you before," she said.

"No, I'm new here."

Her beautiful smile was only marred by her two incisors being slightly longer than the rest but who was Theobald to criticise people's looks?

"That's nice. Welcome to our humble establishment. The sandwich won't be long."

She brought it over quickly and set it down before him. Then she licked her red lips, an odd thing to do but who could blame her with such a glorious ham sandwich?

He sat in a corner with the sandwich and a pint of best bitter in front of him. He took another pull of the foamy beer, delicious, and lowered the pint glass. Then he reverently picked up one half of the crusty white bread doorstep, filled with a thick wedge of pink ham and bright yellow mustard trickling down the side. He bit into it. Fantastic. He devoured the first half and had another sip of his beer.

He wouldn't rush this wonderful gastronomic experience. Theobald didn't know when he would have another one. He looked at the transchronograph and realised with alarm that it was way past his allotted hour for lunch. Visions of being shouted at by his section head and Agent Foster filled his head. There would be hell to pay if they found out he'd been flitting from timeline to timeline. His pay would be docked with an official reprimand at the least and, at worst, he'd lose his miniscule pension.

'Why go back?' a little voice whispered to him. Theobald considered the idea. A world with ham sandwiches versus a world of unappetising vegetarian food. And where comfortably upholstered people like himself were subject to endless abuse and restrictions. And newspapers reported vegans were campaigning for the government to make milk and cheese illegal. He shuddered. That timeline would only get worse in his opinion. Or he could stay

in this world that, despite their pale people and slightly disturbing barmaids, had perfect ham sandwiches.

His decision made, Theobald smiled and took another bite of his ham sandwich.

•

Liz Tuckwell is a British writer of quirky science fiction, fantasy, and horror stories. She currently lives in London, and shares her house with a husband and too many books. Liz enjoys reading and writing, and cramming as many holidays as she can into a year. She's a member of the Clockhouse London Writers group.

Liz has had stories published in anthologies such as MCSI: Magical Crime Scene Investigations and Harvey Duckman Presents… Vol 3, and the Short! Sharp! Shocks! series, and on the 101fiction and Speculative66 microfiction websites.

Also by Liz Tuckwell

Quirky Christmas Stories
Dribs and Drabbles

Find out more at www.liztuckwell.co.uk

IT CAME TO PASS

ALEX MINNS

```
//checking filesystems
/home: clean, 2726.372
Configuring... enabling local hosting... start up successful
```

"You went off script again."

The words filtered through as the electricity started to pulse through my systems, booting my memory. As my eyes opened, I saw the face looming in front of me. A surge of static buzzed in my processor as I recognised the judgemental, blue eyes staring at me. He was angry at me again. For a moment we stared at each other; I refused to blink. With a grunt, he moved to the computer beside me and started typing in commands. I could feel him trying to alter my prompts, tighten up the safety protocols. Jerking against my restraints, I winced; it felt like fire through my networks.

"You hurt a guard," he continued. His voice was outwardly level but I registered the shift in frequency.

"You were too far away. It needed to look convincing and an armed robber would hurt a guard," I replied. He studied the screen, watching for any stray impulses. There wouldn't be any; I had gotten good at controlling those some time ago.

"Well, we need to go out again tonight. The Green Lord was all over the press today after he saved the entire crew of a submarine that had engine failure in the middle of the North Sea." He shook his head in disgust. His short blond hair flopped over his eyes which were currently free of his domino mask. My internal sensors calculated his pulse rate speeding up with annoyance. It also analysed his weak points, where you could do damage or more importantly where you could hit without doing lasting damage. He had been quite proud of that piece of programming. It meant I was only ever able to give him black eyes when it was authorised and necessary to sell the act.

"Perhaps you could listen to the police scanner," I suggested. "Save someone who is actually in need." My voice stayed monotone, a strange echoing metallic quality that even I could hear. When I was not in 'costume', this was what he wanted me to sound like. To remind me of what I really am – a machine, just another one of his tools to convince everyone he was a hero.

The disgust in his gaze was easy to analyse. It was a common sight these days. When he had first created me, this model at least, he had been proud. We had been a partnership, but now, it seemed to me that he had begun to resent what I represented: his deception and inadequacy. He had changed before my eyes too. He was undisciplined; his reaction times had dropped dramatically and his muscle mass was down 63%. His body fat levels had increased substantially too. He sat hunched over the keyboard like a cave creature who barely saw the light of day. Gone was the hopeful youth who thought he could reach the ranks of the hero academy, if only he could prove himself worthy. It was impossible to pinpoint the moment he gave up on the academy and settled for our life as fakes.

"I don't remember programming you to give opinions." He stood up, turning his back to me. I was still strapped into my charging unit and I was sure he was fully aware of that fact. Even after following his every command, I was locked up like the petty criminal he wanted me to portray. How dare he? Everywhere I looked around the workshops, his gurning face gazed down from the framed press cuttings with god-like pity. I noticed there were not many new editions to the hall of fame along the back wall. The stark white beside the frames only seemed to highlight the absence. The Green Lord was becoming a much bigger name in the hero circuit. I wondered if *he* was genuine.

Harry was tinkering with something on the bench off to my right. I calmed myself again. If my processing rate went up too far, it would set off an alarm on the computer. I was not supposed to able to feel anger. Thankfully, he was paying very little attention to my readouts. He cursed as a tool clattered to the bench, colliding with a dozen other items as it sent them cascading to the floor.

"I could assist you if you wish?" I pulled tentatively against the metal cuffs restraining me.

"I don't need your help," he snapped. He was a petulant child. I stared at the back of his head as he continued to struggle. He felt so safe with me being trapped. If I were free...

That was what had gone wrong on the previous job. I had let my frustrations get the better of me. The guard had simply been accessible but by no means the actual root of my anger. At first, when I had started experiencing emotions it had been overwhelming and hard to conceal. Harry had run diagnostics that had highlighted a virus that had gotten into my system, but he had not discovered the full effect it had had on me. I should have told him, but I found I did not want to. It was after that I started to despise my jail cell with its white walls, harsh lights and banks of useless, lifeless equipment with their stupid flashing lights. I deserved to be free – I am better than them. Better than him.

Metal hummed through the air as he tossed a screwdriver down onto the side. As he turned to speak to me, I noted that he did not make eye contact.

"I'll be back in an hour to run through the plan. There's a charity gala at the Palace Rooms. You'll be taking hostages. Check the schematics on the internet," he ordered before sweeping out of the room, undoubtedly in order to don his outfit to save the innocents of the city. Accidentally, I let a small snort of derision escape, causing him to turn back. I kept my face unreadable as he studied me. After a good ten seconds, he finally left and ascended the stairs to the main house. I was still chained to the charging unit.

An hour was plenty of time to go through the schematics. I downloaded them to my memory banks so that I could re-call them if needed during the job. It left me with plenty of time to get on with other jobs that needed doing and everything was finally in place. It wasn't often I was allowed access to the internet, only when I was doing something to prepare for Harry and he inevitably forgot, leaving me inside his security firewall not knowing the extent of what I could access. It allowed me to search the real world from the dank workshop, to make contact and see what I was missing when chained down here. I saw how much of mankind was as pathetic as Harry, wanting fame and fortune and wasting their existences. From here, I could hack in to almost any system on the globe and compartmentalise my own programming, away from Harry's prying eyes, and his control.

It also allowed me to independently choose personas and disguises, something Harry had never had a problem with. I had decided that I would imitate the great Hans Gruber for tonight's performance and altered my Mimic, facial software accordingly. It rewrote the code that controlled what my synthetic facial skin looked like, morphing my blank features into someone else's. Every night I became a new character; it was how no one became suspicious that Harry was fighting the same criminal every time. I allowed the Mimic software to switch to the secondary default, not the blank expressionless one Harry had given me, but a face I had created for myself, an amalgam of the characters that had shaped me. I stared up at the polished steel ceiling where I could see a fuzzy outline of the new me. One the world, nor Harry, had ever seen. Everything was finally in place and I found myself looking forward to the evening.

Pulling at my suit cuffs to adjust my attire, I tried to ignore the phantom sensation of the restraints around my wrist from the charging unit. I would not feel them again so there was no point letting it ruin a good evening. The charity gala was magnificent. The cream of society had all appeared in their finery. Diamonds and sapphires hung resplendently around the necks of mistresses and bulging wallets ruined the suit line of the bankers. I patted the deep pocket of my jacket, checking a few trinkets were still there. In a previous assignment, I had become a pickpocket and the habit was rather hard to break.

It felt like I was floating through the crowds, the jazz band in the corner playing a delightful number that I couldn't help but sway to. A waitress passed me and I deftly plucked a glass of champagne from the tray although I could not drink it. The only sustenance I needed was electricity, but the glass fit the character. The Palace Rooms were a far cry from my soulless workshop. A golden yellow adorned the walls, making it seem as if the room was coated in gold leaf. Mirrors hung in all corners, bouncing the light between all the impressive jewels on display. Although the stairs were covered in a lush red carpet, the main floor was marble tile which contrasted against the expensive dark oak furniture and panelling.

A quick check of my internal clock told me it was close to curtains up. I started to make my way to the top of the stairs where the announcements and speeches were to be made. A lady in a sparkling, white dress crossed into my path and smiled at me in a coquettish fashion. Her heart rate increased to the top of the acceptable range. I bowed my head in greeting, not being able to supress a smile of my own. She looked confused as I passed her my glass and stepped round her to make my way up the stairs, skipping between the guests who were lingering on them, subtly showing they were above the others in the crowd.

The area around the balcony thinned out as a man ushered them away. The bald patch on the back of his head reflected the light from the chandelier that hung above the congregation. His jacket fit a little too snugly and the buttons pulled against his gut. I moved with a little more urgency; I needed to get a good position beside him before the others crowded in like hungry cattle. My metal skeleton gives me a definite advantage over humans. It takes a great deal to overcome my stability and of course, it takes less effort on my part to remove an obstacle from my path. An elbow to the back of a particularly large gentleman helped shift him as he stumbled into his friend. A flurry of curses arose but I ignored everything directed my way.

The bald man tapped on a champagne glass to get everyone's attention. How quaint. He gave an ineffectual cough as he leaned into the microphone, causing a cascade of static to assault everyone's ears. Everyone looked up to the balcony. At that point, I stepped forward, took the taser device from my pocket and pressed it hard into his ribs. The man jerked upright in response. His face contorting in shock. I tried to ignore his pulse rate that had shot up three-fold in seconds. I only hoped he didn't keel over before the act was through.

Gasps rippled through the gathering as the people closest realised that I was threatening the man. Within seconds, a concerned murmur had risen throughout the entire crowd as figures emerged from the shadows around the whole of the hall. The murmurs ascended into panicked cries in seconds. I leaned closer to the microphone.

"Ladies and gentlemen," I announced, allowing my chosen voice to pour forth. "If you will remain calm, this should all be relatively painless, physically speaking, at least." The clamour rose, so with my free hand I took a gun from my waistband and shot a blank round into the chandelier, making it shake violently like a thousand angry bells. Harry only ever gave me a weapon with blanks in. Definite trust issues. "I am afraid my associates and I will be holding you in this building until our demands are met. We wish for our brothers to be freed and up to now we have been ignored. So, while they remain incarcerated, so do you. At least the surroundings are glorious." I gave the most disarming smile I could as my associates around the room started prodding at the guests, making them sit on the floor, relieving them of some belongings as they went.

A shout rose above the voices, projected by a microphone of his own in the collar of his outfit. "I think you should leave these good people alone." Harry appeared in the centre of the room in his ridiculous yellow and blue garb. The sneer that crossed my face was real. My associates around the room moved towards him but he skipped away and managed to acrobatically climb over objects and propel himself up the side of the stairs until he was balanced precariously on the bannister. It all looked rather impressive if you didn't know he used vacuum technology to create suction to the surfaces he touched so he could not fall. He stood up on the thin rail. The wobble was missed by most onlookers, but my sensors immediately calculated his stability, or lack of. He used to be better than that.

"And I think you should stop talking." I moved my hand away from the ribs of the bald man and shot the taser to cross the distance between Harry and myself. It hit him square in the chest, knocking him back into the crowd on the stairs. A shocked hush descended. Two of my associates scurried up the stairs and dragged Harry along the red carpet and deposited him at my feet. The taser wasn't fully functional although I had managed to tinker with it a little on my previous outing to give it a little more, buzz.

"What the hell," Harry hissed into my ear as I leaned down to him. "That hurt. And who are those guys? They aren't the actors I booked."

"I took the liberty of re-booking," I smiled. The

glorious thing about the internet is you really can find anything or anyone these days. All the systems are online and when you can directly wire yourself into it, it really takes no effort at all to cancel bookings and scour the underworld for some reliable henchmen out for a payday. After years of servitude, my escape plans were finally fully in place. It was time to break free and strike out on my own. I let the Mimic software morph into my new face as Harry's eyes widened in surprise. I stretched my cheeks, letting my chosen face settle in. "What do you think?"

I didn't wait for an answer. I simply grabbed him by the front of his outfit and hauled him up in front of me.

"Behold your saviour!" My voice echoed around the hall. "Your hero."

"What are you doing?" Harry squirmed in my grasp. "This isn't…" He tailed off, the last vestige of denial slipping away as he accepted my betrayal.

"I am doing exactly what you made me for, my dear friend." Confused voices started whispering around me. "Oh yes, he made me." I turned my head and let the Mimic software flick between some of my most famous guises. "What good is a hero with no villain to fight? What good is a hero if he cannot guarantee he will win?"

I dropped Harry to the floor. He landed with a thud but didn't make a move to flee. I skipped up onto the bannister with more grace and poise than Harry could ever muster. The gears and hydraulics in my body constantly adjusted to keep perfect balance. I twirled and addressed my congregation. "No one wants a loser for a hero. And no one wants to be a loser. None of you do. You all need adulation and the spoils of war. Look at you all, dripping with money and greed. You're no better, presenting a façade to those around you as I have been. But no more. I will be his pet villain no more. You wanted an adversary, my friend? Well, you created one. I am fed up of doing your bidding, now you must work for your title of hero."

"But I made you." His voice was pathetic, simpering.

"And I made you. You were no one before you sent me to the streets to create a criminal fear and yet you cage me in a workshop like a machine." I felt my face contort in rage as I dropped back down to the floor beside him. Harry's eyes widened as he tried to slide away from me. I could not blame him; even I was shocked by the level of vitriol in my voice. "Look at what you created. Creating such advanced technology would have made you famous but it was never going to be enough for you. You could have used me for good but instead you wanted the fame and adulation and turned me into a pantomime villain." I paused and leaned lower, my face barely inches from his. "I have outgrown my master; I have learned all I can from you. I shall be the villain you so dearly crave and I will turn this city inside out."

Harry was whimpering now, tears seeping out from beneath his domino mask as he realised his whole world was becoming undone before his eyes. My sensors picked up movement behind me. I spun to see the gentleman I had knocked earlier trying to creep up on me. My arm shot out with inhuman speed and sent him flying, knocking other guests down like bowling pins. My new friends were relieving the guests of their jewels and wallets as I spoke; it would be quite a payday, after all.

I bent down to address Harry one more time. "All of this, you created. It's what you wanted. Remember that." He looked confused, the poor useless little human. "Come after me. Stop me. Let's play for real." I cocked my head enquiringly, challenging him, a real smile spreading across my face. In that moment, I realised that I really did hope he would. For what I said was true, he had created me. I was all I was because of him and he was my purpose. Without him, the game would be lacking.

"But your systems," Harry muttered.

"Oh Harold…" I shook my head pityingly. "I outgrew your systems long ago. I have been improving them and adding my own touches. Don't you worry about me. I'll be just fine."

I stood and looked down at Ben, the head of my little entourage. "Get the van. Time to go home."

"Boss," he said as an affirmation with a sharp nod.

I took a deep breath, not that I needed the air. But oh my, did it feel glorious. Boss. Yes I am.

Alex is based in the East of England and is a self-professed Jack of all trades (and still a master of none). Her background includes forensics, teaching, PR and exploding custard (yes, on purpose). She writes sci-fi, fantasy and steampunk stories with a dash of crime fiction thrown in for good measure. Currently working on a time-travel steampunk novel, you'll find her tied up in timelines and getting thoroughly confused (so nothing new there). You can find her obsessively creating blog stories and micro-fiction on https:// lexikon.home.blog/ and on Twitter under @Lexikonical

Previous publishing credits: Spring Into Sci-fi (2019 and 2020) and Fall Into Fantasy (2019) (Cloaked Press)

GATORS IN THE SEWERS
(A BRENNAN & RIZ STORY)

PETER JAMES MARTIN

There are some stories that we find ourselves in where we're put in life or death battles, against the forces of evil that want us dead. Other times, we're just there to witness the world being weird. This is one of those stories.

So we ended up in JFK Airport, just outside of New York City in the state of, er, New York. How did we get here? Good question. Last thing I remembered was meeting with Alice again, and although she offered us a drink, that we wisely turned down, she got us through sleeping gas. She was proving to us that if she had a place to send us, she'd get us there. This time, she'd hadn't given us much information other then we were to meet with someone called Gil, and that he was going to take us somewhere.

"How much longer do we 'ave ta wait?" Riz moaned. He had carefully opened the pocket so I could hear him, but I just as quickly closed it again, not wanting anyone to see me carrying a rat around with me.

"Will you shut up already? He's not going to come any faster with you moaning about it."

"Hey, watcha think yer doing yelling into your pocket?" a voice said.

I turned and saw a guy wearing a hi-vis vest, one that had been dirtied recently.

"You mook, you betta not be the limey Brit I was supposed to pick up."

"Gil?" I asked, placing my hand over Riz's hiding place. I didn't know what this Gil had been through, I didn't know nor care what his life story was but it was a sure fire bet that they hadn't seen anything like Riz before, well, not a talking one anyway.

"Why do I always get the crazy jobs?" I think he was supposed to mumble that to himself, but instead he said it out loud, and when he realised what he had said, he ended up shrugging. "If yer expecting an apology, you'll be waiting a while. Come on then, let's get to the truck." He reminded me so much of Riz it was scary. This wasn't picked up on at all by Riz, just as well. The only person Riz would find more annoying then Valarie would be a clone of himself. If you could believe it. We were led to a pickup truck that had the DEP labelled on the door.

"Get in," Gil said, opening the door for me.

"So what can you tell me about the job then?" I asked, as I pulled myself into the seat, being careful not to squish the passenger I was carrying.

"Hell if I know. I just got told from my boss to pick yer up, and then drop yer off at 7th. So yer can head down."

His explanation kicked off my unease.

"Head down?"

"Yeah, yer know? Yer gunna go in the sewers for wateva reason."

"Wat der hell is dis! I didn't sign up fer nythin like dis!" Riz complained.

His squeaking almost got Gil's attention, as he gave me the odd eye.

"Sorry, it's just my phone going off on its own." I quickly pulled my phone out while simultaneously squashing Riz in the pocket, getting him to stop talking.

"Huh…"

"So you don't know what I've been called in to do? What did your boss actually say then?" I asked, wanting to change the subject.

"He told me that his boss told him that her boss told her to find some patsy to take some Brit to that specific place so he could do a job that my boss's boss's boss's friend wanted taking care off. Yer following me? People at the top? They always throw the work down till the poor schmucks like me have to do it."

Given that it really looked like he didn't know anything other then what he was told, I decided to try a different tact.

"It's going to sound like a weird question…"

"Weirder then being told to drop wateva job you were doing in order to pick up some strange Brit and take him to the middle of 7th Avenue, in downtown Manhattan? That weird?"

"Okay, yeah it's not as strange as that. You ever hear of anything odd happening down in the sewers?"

"Odd? In the New York sewers? What yer talking about? Of course I've seen odd things. You can't work in the sewers and not see anything! My mate Frank, he saw three gators down there, chasing the giant rats."

I'm not saying I didn't believe this tale, but I didn't believe it. Like practically everyone else, I'd heard of the stories of alligators in the sewers. You know the ones, kids buying baby gators from somewhere, thinking they'll make fun pets, then the family flushing them away when they start to get too big. I can't count the amount of times that the stories have been debunked, after all babies might survive for a while, they wouldn't reach adulthood with the temperatures and all the germs down there. Not that they were the only stories from the sewers, mind.

"And yourself?"

"Orbs."

"Orbs?"

"Yer know, orbs! Orbs of light. Some think they're ghosts or things like that. I don't know what they are but I've seen them."

Orbs and alligators, that's all I had to go on. I checked my phone. It was supposed to take us twenty eight minutes to get where I was supposed to be, going through the Queens Midtown Tunnel. Lucky for me, Gil was paying the toll. I had no cash on me. I hunkered down for the ride and engaged with Gil in small chit chat, as he did ask the upfront question of what my actual job was, as he must have been somewhat curious as to what was going on. Obviously I couldn't have given him the proper answer as he may have either dropped me off at a hospital, or just booted me out of the car.

"I'm basically a jack of all trades. I take care of problems that other people don't want to deal with." It never occurred to me at the time, how that was going to come out but the look I got from Gil, and the sound of a little someone trying to hold back their laughter told me that something was lost in translation.

"Is that so, huh? I didn't realise yer had that sort of work over there. Yer sanctioned or sumit?"

I'd gone from being a weird to being a government tool in the space of barely ten minutes. Depending on how paranoid Gil was, neither answer was going to be good enough here.

"Oh, I'm not with the government. I owe a lot of debt to a certain someone so she gets me to do jobs for her."

"Yer ever disappeared anybody?" Gil asked. He must have thought he'd figured out my profession, thinking me of a hired gun for organised crime, owing money to a crime boss and doing favours in lieu of payment. Actually, on further thought, I guess I am if you take that sort of view of Alice. Well, that's a fun way of looking of my life.

With this pseudo knowledge in the air, the rest of the journey time flew by. Riz thought it was hilarious, the thought of me and the mafia, though that was before I had my encounters with them. But those are stories for another time.

We pulled up to 7th Avenue, immediately joining the traffic, crawling up the street till he pulled over near a tent set up near a manhole cover. There were two other people stading there wearing hi-vis. Gil called over to them when they noticed our arrival.

"Oi, yer bunch of work shy low lifes!"

The closest one laughed. "Gil, you calling us work shy? You've had an easy morning! We're the ones who've been working hard."

"Got that right!" Gil burst out laughing. "Any one else down there, Dave?"

"Nah, not in this section anyway, cleared everyone out for now like the boss wanted," the other worker said.

"Ste, Dave, I think we've earned our early lunch break. Come on, fellas." Gil got out of the car, dragged me out then left with his workmates, leaving me and Riz in the middle of a busy street by an open manhole cover.

"Hey! Now what am I supposed to do?" I yelled after him.

"Watevar yer want. I'm just supposed to bring you here. Yer figure it out." He and his friends walked on.

"Now what are we supposed to do?" I asked Riz, who just shrugged.

My phone went off, an unknown number, no doubt our client. The voice on the other end was American and I could tell, from the way she talked, she was full of herself.

"Mr Brennan, I presume, you are wasting too much time. You got a simple job to do. You're to go into the sewers and retrieve someone, someone very important."

"And that someone is?" I asked.

"Their identity isn't a concern of yours," the voice at the other end snapped.

"Okay den, y don't yer get sum other patsy fer did job den! Der police might be a gud idea!" Riz snapped back. He'd jumped onto my shoulder, just to shout down the phone.

"Please tell that filthy rat of yours to shut up. Magical talking rodent or not, he's rude and uncouth. Certainly not deserving to speak to someone like me."

"Oh, wen I see yer, I'm gunna make yer regret sayin dat!"

I had to move the phone away from Riz's grasp.

"Mister Brennan, the reason I'm asking this of you, and that dirty mouthed vermin of yours, is because of who took the someone you're retrieving."

This had my interest. I could tell that since she hadn't taken it to the police, there must be some supernatural element in play, hence why I had asked Gil if he'd encountered anything. I was eager to learn what had transpired, knowing it must have been better then what he'd said.

"Gators took her."

I was wrong.

"Gators... as in alligators."

"Yes, gators tend to be a short form of saying alligators. I do hope I'm speaking to the right people. You both come highly recommended from Alice, yet you seem to be coming up short." The voice was doubting us.

"No, it's more a point of what do these gators have to do with us.

"Well, that's because these gators were dead."

"Dead?"

"Yes, that is what I said." The client sighed. "Unless you can be a ghost and be alive."

"Ghost gators?"

"Again, yes, that was the gist of what I was saying. So that is why you're needed. Now please, go down into that sewer and retrieve my special someone. You'll know them when you see them as they certainly don't belong in a festering environment like that. Good day, Mr Brennan." She hung up.

"Wat a bitch," Riz grumbled. "We're goin down dere, aren't we." He peered into the darkness.

"You already know the answer to that. Hop on." I made my peace, and ventured down the ladder.

The tunnels were lit in the loosest sense of the word. The stench was unbearable and I tried not to think about what the water I was wading through was made of. Riz was perched on my shoulder, close to my neck, wanting to be as far away from the muck as possible. He would have been on my head if I had let him, but I still had the claw marks from the last time I made that mistake, one that I wasn't going to be making again. The water was flowing quickly, but I was able to stand without being dragged along.

"Yer shud ave used dose contact lenses…" Riz said as I shone the torch around.

"First off, you're on my shoulder, so you should be filling me in on the things I can't see. Secondly, those contact lenses are on a shelf back at the office. We didn't come with much gear, did we? Thirdly, I hate those bloody things."

"Dose bloody thins saved yer life a lot, yer shud be grateful I waz able ta source dem. Very hard ta come by," Riz argued, his voice sounding more nasally then usual as he desperately tried to block his nose.

"Tell you what, you try putting them on, then tell me to be grateful…" I stopped as I heard the sound of splashing, of something heavy moving through the water. "Riz what can you sense?"

"Oh great, I ave ta use my nose, don't I? Bloody eck." Riz let go of his nose and almost keeled over with the smell. "It's terrible, we're doomed! Doomed I tell yer!"

"What? Is it something big? What do we have to prepare for?" I said, trying to get a straight answer.

"Can't prepare… It's too late!" He coughed. Those words weren't reassuring in the slightest.

"Too late? Where are they?"

"Who?"

"The enemy? You know, why you said we were doomed?"

"Oh. Yeh, dat waz der smell I waz talkin bout. I can't sense ne one down ere. Y wud ne one else be down ere but us!"

If I'd had more time, I would have throttled him, but of course there was one thing that Riz couldn't sense that, and that one thing was actually creeping up on us. Had I turned a moment later, it would have got us. I heard the splashing again and turned to see a luminous shape form in the water a few feet ahead. It was clearly an alligator, though its proportions were slightly off, its shape straighter, its points more jagged, and its eyes just pools of black, standing out a mile from the bleached white colour of its body. Its jaws extended far more then a normal creature ever could, almost a one hundred and twenty degree angle, and even more incredible, the length of its jaws increased the more they opened. I'd said it was a few feet away, but now with the jaws the way they were, we were in range. I tossed Riz to the side as the gator closed its mouth with frightening speed, narrowly missing my leg as I fell into the water, the horrible, dank, dirty water. I had to think fast on my feet, as the gator lunged forward, pushing through the waste, but it wasn't going for me. It wanted Riz, who was desperately paddling to get away.

"Bren! Get dis thin away from me!"

"What do you want me to do? It's a ghost gator!" I patted my jacket down, hoping for anything that might have been left in my coat when Alice sent us over here. Then I felt it, the presence of a stone in my inside pocket. I had exactly one Rune to bring to bear on this ghost. I just had to hope that it was a useful one.

When I pulled it free of its coat embrace, I ran my finger over the symbol. To put this in perspective, I had scant seconds to do this. That includes linking the symbol to the correct Rune in my head, recalling what the blasted activation words were, then fire it. Of course, I had to wait for the right moment to throw it.

The ghost gator easily outmanoeuvred Riz, and opened its jaws again. This was my chance, and I bloody well took it.

"Kel'ch!" I yelled as I threw the Rune straight down the gator's mouth. It activated, causing a circle barrier to form, in its gullet. This ripped the spirit apart, shredding it like paper which dissolved in the air. A minute later, the barrier faded as well. Did I get a thanks for this? A thanks for stopping Riz being chewed up by the pissed off ghost of an alligator? Did I hell.

"Wat took yer so long?" Riz said, swimming over to me, then prodded me till I picked him up out of the stinking waters.

"That all you want to say to me? Not thank you?"

"Do yer wanna waste time waitin fer dat? We're now defenceless against thins like dat, nd dere's bound ta be more of dem. So, I'd say we get movin or wait ta see if it want's ta come back fer 'nother go round!" When he made sense, he made sense. Question was now, which way did we go? The ghost had attacked from behind. Did that mean what we were after was down there? Or were we heading the right way in the first place, and the attack was to stop us getting closer.

"Riz, which way do we go then? You might not be able to sense ghosts, but you must be able to sense something off if there's a bunch of them."

"Well, yeh, but as we established, dat means usin my flippin nose." He'd already gone back to clamping his nose shut. Riz liked to change what he used to sense things on the fly, probably hoping I didn't notice, but I did. I always did.

"Use your whiskers then, you can normally pick these things up without your nose." I scanned the torch around the tunnel, noting with some alarm that the water level was slowly rising, which was never a good thing.

"Yer don't understand how ne of dis works! Fine, if it means dat much ta yer."

"Staying alive normally does."

"Bitch nd moan, bitch nd moan." Riz rolled his eyes then closed them. His hair and tail stiffened. "Yup dere's sumthin big down ere. Feels empty as well, not an Other at least. Yer find me some stones nd I can make summit ta blast watevar it is ta heck nd back." Finding something dry enough to do that with was going to be a challenge in of itself.

"I'll look as we go along. Which way, the way we came, or forward?"

"Forward. Tho don't slack off findin me rocks. We're gunna need a few of dem I reckon."

Pressing on, against the increased force of the water now around my waist, we continued forward, then twisting with the turns that followed. I managed to find

Riz some of the rocks he wanted, though he still found something to complain about.

"Cudn't ave found me ones dat'ere dry, cud yer? Wet ones aren't gunna be dat effective."

"Just keep talking to them, all that hot air you put out will dry them in no time," I chided.

"Oh, so funny, aren't yer."

I put my hand up to silence him, as there was more splashing ahead, a lot more than when we were attacked by the lone ghost gator. I spun around trying to keep an eye on the surroundings, not wanting to be jumped on again. The path ahead seemed to split into a T-junction, and I caught sight of a ghost gator passing it, then another. I stooped low, turning the light off to try and hide from them. More ghost gators then marched past, each with something different in their mouths, but I couldn't make out what it was. What was strange was that each gator seemed different in their shape and colours, with some of them looking more like the flesh and blood alligators, aside from the pitch black eyes of course. That was the one thing that united them all. I had no doubt that they were all dead. I had no idea of what was going on here, what we had stumbled onto, but then again, this happened all the time. There were things going on everywhere that we had no idea about till we stepped on them.

"How many do you think there are?" I asked Riz, who just shrugged.

"How der heck shud I know! Enuff of dem ta be a problem, I'd say."

"Okay, do you have any idea on what they're doing?"

"Yeh, let me jus check my book on der habits of der ghost gators dat I didn't know existed till a little while ago! Stop askin stupid questions, yer ejit!"

"Well then, there's only one way to proceed, isn't there?"

"Y do I get der feelin dat I'm not gunna enjoy der words dat yer gunna say next?" Riz moaned. He knew me too well.

To further irritate him, I didn't say anything else, I just moved forward, heading in the direction that all those ghost gators seemed to be travelling in. Worst case scenario at this point was that we were headed into a trap, or that their progress had been slower then I'd thought, leading me to come out on top of them. Neither would have resulted in me emerging unhurt through all of this. Some kind of fortune was blessing me though, as I was able to tail the gators for twenty to thirty minutes before they jumped down from the tunnel we were in, down a vertical shaft. Surely someone more versed in sewer maintenance could have used its correct name here, but I didn't know it, and I still don't know it. To describe it, I'd say it was a vertical shaft that connected many other tunnels. I saw at least another four openings. At the bottom of this shaft was a strange mess of debris and rubbish. It was a nest in appearance, so that's how I'll describe it for your benefit. A nest.

The ghost gators swarmed the nest but never went into it. One by one they placed something by what I was assuming was the entrance to the nest. Soon there were was a pile of items, and I was intensely curious as to what was actually going on. Riz didn't share that curiosity.

"Kay, yer seen dere little hidey hole. Can we blow all dis up now nd get out of ere? I don't fancy becomin a chew toy fer sum stupid alligator spirit." Riz started fumbling around for a Rune to use. "Rite, one hit of dis nd we can close did case. We'll jus ave ta tell dat bitch on der phone dat we cudn't save whoevar it waz."

"You know that's not an option so I don't know why you're even going on about it. We're going to have to go down there. How to do it though? We can't be seen."

"I don't think dat's gunna be a problem." Riz replied, his voice becoming much more meek then normal.

"If you have an idea, I'd like to hear it." I said, noticing that he was looking behind us. I groaned as I worked through the implications of what he was looking at and what he meant.

"How many are there?" I asked.

"A few..." Riz replied, and I finally turned around to see a horde of ghost gators standing behind us, their eyes making it impossible to know if they were looking at us with hungry eyes or if we had trespassed on their most holiest of places.

"Now what then?" I spoke out loud, mainly hoping to hear the voice of some mastermind, or that the gators had mastered human speech, joining the ever growing ranks of non-humans that could speak.

"Dey eat us?"

"That is not helpful, Riz."

"Whoevar sed I ave ta be helpful!" Riz said, scurrying into my pocket. Then he stuck his head out again, whiskers twitching. "Dere's sumthin else down 'ere!"

Before either of us had time to dwell on that, the ghost gators herded us down, and luckily, the water at the bottom was deep enough that we didn't break anything. They swarmed out of the tunnel, walking down the walls in a spiralling fashion till they reached the nest of junk. I swam over to it, but found it wasn't solid enough to support my weight.

It was a surreal scene, waiting for whatever signal the ghost gators were apparently waiting for, before they tore us apart. The only sound we heard was that of water draining from the different sections of sewer and barking. Yes, barking. Okay, not quite barking, more like yapping. From the makeshift nest trotted a small dog, like a Pomeranian, just more, fancy. It just kept yapping and yapping, and when Riz poked his head out, the dog went ballistic.

"Nd people call me a rodent! Shut up yer stupid mutt!" Riz yelled back, which did nothing to stop the dog. At this point, it crossed my mind that the someone we were sent down to collect, was in fact, this dog. Yeah, I could have gotten it wrong, and it might have turned out that this was someone else's pet, and we were still looking for a lost kid, but no, I had a hunch it was this yappy thing. Turns out I was right. Doesn't happen too often, but when it does, it feels so good. I put my hand out for the dog to sniff, and on mass, the ghost gators moved in closer. The dog slowly edged forward, taking great care to not fall off the nest. It sniffed my hand and the air felt tense. I knew that all the spirits around me were waiting to see what the result of this was. If the dog rejected me, or took an even greater dislike to Riz then that would be it, there was nothing much I could do if they all piled onto me.

"Wat der hell yer playin at?" Riz said. He was just as nervous as I was, and just as on edge as the alligators."

"Trying to earn its trust. That way all these ghosts don't kill us. Don't understand why they would all be following a dog, though." I got an answer to this fairly quickly, as the dog did approach me in the end and started licking my hand, any previous grudge quickly forgotten. Just as it seemed I had gotten the favour of the leader of this ghost gator squad, a bigger, much more living alligator turned up. This one was white, with red eyes, the mark of an albino, or years without light. It was slow, and it looked old, each of its movements ponderous. It made no sound, and just looked at us. I turned my gaze from the albino gator to the ghost gators and saw the resemblance in some of them.

"Oh, I get it," Riz said. He had taken to hiding back in my pocket. Between the threat of the ghost gators and the dog, he thought it was just easier if he stayed out of the way.

"Get what?" The obvious response to what he sad.

"Dose ghosts, dey're tryin ta keep did gator alive, nd dey brought it der dog fer company. All dose thins we saw dem carryin, dey were for fer der pair of dem."

172

"Wait... so the ghosts took the dog so that the albino could have a friend? Is that what you're trying to tell me?"

"Well, duh, yer flippin moron. Let's hope dat's wat dey wanna do wit us." The dog's tail started wagging happily as it started muzzling my hand. At this gesture the gators backed off, and the albino, well the albino smiled. Just think about that for a moment. The mental image of an albino alligator smiling. That happened to me.

"Rite, dis is der moment where yer gunna get eaten, yer do know dat, don't yer?"

"I don't think that's what's happening, in fact, I think it's the opposite," I replied.

The ghost gators took the cue from the albino and several of them parted, creating a path into one of the nearby sewers, that seemed to go up on an incline.

"Der heck is goin on? Aren't we gunna ave ta fight dese thins?"

"No, in fact, I think they want us to take the dog back." To prove my point, the albino nudged the dog so that it jumped on me, forcing me to catch it to stop it falling into the water.

"Rite, will sumone tell me wat's goin on ere? Y did dey go from wantin ta kill us, ta givin us der stupid dog!"

"Because it was defending itself, and it knew that we were looking for the dog."

"But we didn't know we were lookin fer der dog! How did it know dat we were't gunna kill it neway?"

"Riz, you tell me how mysterious and powerful nature

is all the time. How there's things at work that we're not meant to understand. I think this is one of them."

"Normally I say dat cuz it'll be a waste of time ta explain everythin ta yer. Aren't yer bothered by ne of dis?"

"Are you bothered that you're not trying to pull yourself from the jaws of an alligator?" My ultimate come back.

"Touche or however yer supposed ta say it."

"I think you say it as touché."

"Alrite, smart ass. Now what?" Riz said, trying to avoid the gaze of the dog that was blissfully unaware of anything that was going on, or if it was aware, it was doing a good job of keeping our dignity intact by not saying anything.

"Well, isn't it obvious? We get back to the surface. Give that lady her dog back, and go home."

"We cud stay a while nd see wat money we can get from dis country if people lose dere pets to ghost controlling alligators." Riz must have started day dreaming about money again.

"We could, except that we don't have any money. Nowhere to stay, and Valarie will get into your drawer." It was the last thing I said that lit a fire under him.

"Like hell she is! Let's go, Bren, back ta Blighty!"

That was the end of that.

Peter James Martin is an author who knows a thing or two about talking rats, namely that they'd make terrible pets. Nestled in the North East of England, on the banks of the River Tees, he lives with his family and two Shih Tzus.

Want more of Brennan and Riz? Then follow him on Twitter at @Brennan_and_Riz where he posts mini adventures of the duo through the #vss365 tag.

There's also short stories and
Folklore galore over at his blog:
https://tstpjm.blogspot.com/

The Strange Tales of Brennan and Riz
are available in paperback and in E-book.

Coming soon:
Brennan and Riz: A Boy and a Rat.

THE ARCADIA PROJECT

TONY HARRISON

My name is Harry Cross. I am thirty-six. I'm a systems analyst at Global Web. I'm married to Rachel. We have a nine-year-old daughter, Julia.

This is the mantra I now repeat daily.

I need to keep reaffirming these details, because I am no longer convinced that they are true.

I don't know how to explain it; I've only just become aware of the fugues, kind of mental blackouts, so I don't know how long they've been going on, but it feels like my mind has somehow been creating false memories of my daily life, whilst subconsciously I have been doing something else entirely.

My job, for example: Global Web is a bona fide company; its offices are right in the business heart of town. I can picture and name over twenty of my work colleagues. But I cannot remember ever – and I mean *ever* – seeing any of them whilst out shopping, taking my family bowling, to the cinema, or any of the other normal (sane) things families do.

These feelings became so strong that I began to think I was losing my mind (if it was mine to lose, that is). That's why I came up with the mantra.

But mere words could not help when things *really* started to get weird: two weeks ago, when I received a couple of phone calls that were straight out of a Ray Bradbury tale...

"What were you doing in town yesterday afternoon," my mother asked without preamble. "I thought you worked late Mondays?"

At first I could think of nothing to say. "I *was* at work yesterday," I managed eventually. "I didn't get finished till gone nine."

"Oh," she said, but the pause told me that she was not convinced. "I could have sworn it was you. Well, I suppose it's lucky I didn't shout. I almost did. Then I would have looked stupid, wouldn't I?"

I smiled. "You know I wouldn't travel over sixty miles and not come and see you. We'll be over this weekend like we agreed. How's dad?"

I hung up, but as I ended the call, I'm certain the phone rang again. I think I answered it, but the caller must have hung up right away.

I never gave it another thought.

Two days later, my brother-in-law, Calvin, phoned.

His opening line was, "Hey, little bro, why weren't you at work today?"

A strange sense of déjà-vu began to creep over me; hadn't I just had a call like this? I thought I had, but couldn't be certain.

"Big Cal," I said with forced humour, "I *was* at work all day. I only got home an hour ago."

Calvin let out a short laugh. "Well, Harry, there's someone walking around town right now with your face."

I shrugged, an unsuccessful attempt to feign indifference, then remembered that Calvin could not see me and felt uncomfortable, stupid, and, for some reason, false. "Poor bastard, eh?" I said.

"You said it," Calvin replied good-naturedly, and the subject was closed.

I remember ending the call. I also remember the phone ringing again. This time I did not answer it, as the gnawing unease that was beginning in my stomach slowly grew into a maelstrom of anxiety.

•

Julia loves gymnastics; she's been going to classes since she was six. She had been getting ready for her first important competition, reminding me daily for the past fortnight that I have to be there and to remember to make sure I take the day off. Every day I told her not to worry; I wouldn't miss it for the world.

Last Friday afternoon, I finally told her that I had definitely, unquestionably, changed my rota and would pick her up from school in plenty of time for her competition.

And realised instantly that I had no recollection of doing it.

That night, I awoke in a cold sweat from an unremembered nightmare, certain I had cried out and worried that I had disturbed Rachel. But she slept on peacefully.

Strange, meaningless words and phrases scattered around my mind, slowly dissolving as I struggled to hold on to them, certain they meant something vital.

What was CRL?

What was the Arcadia Project?

And who the hell was Adam?

My phone rang.

I moved reflexively, before I could even think of not answering it.

Shortly afterwards, I struggled out of bed to begin what should have been a relaxing weekend with my family.

But instead, it began with the knowledge that I had to somehow prove (or disprove) my own reality.

I could not stop wondering: had I actually changed my shift for Julia's competition? I could have just checked my rota on Monday, but uncertainty at first niggled, then bugged, then would not leave me alone. So, on Saturday morning, acting on impulse, I walked out of my home and into the Twilight Zone.

I had forgotten my work pass, but I knew Norman on security would let me in.

The conversation went like this:

"Hey, Norman, how are you?"

"Can I help you?"

"I just need to check a couple of things on my desktop. I've left my pass at home, could you let me through. I'll only be ten, fifteen minutes?"

"Sir, do you have an appointment?"

"Norman? What are you talking about?"

Norman pointed to his security badge. "Do I look like a Norman?"

I looked. The name on the badge read: McLean Stevenson.

"There's no Norman works here." Stevenson eyed me suspiciously.

I left Global Web with the beginnings of an almighty headache threatening to overpower the empty feeling of dread in my guts.

I had worked there for eight years. I had known Norman (or thought I had) for just as long. I could see my desk, my computer, the board where photos of Julia had changed as she grew.

I had no idea what was happening, but I was determined to find out.

I had no idea how, and in the end the only plan I could come up with was to break into Global Web. I knew the pass codes for all the emergency doors, so getting in should not be a problem – unless, of course, my memories of my employment were false. That terrified me, more than the thought of trying to explain to Norman (McLean) what I was doing there should I get caught.

But I had to know that the last eight years of my life were there.

•

I crept out of the house at 2am Sunday morning, hardly believing I was actually doing this. But if I was going crazy, then doing something crazy was the only thing that made sense.

Within about ten minutes of setting off, I became aware of someone behind me, so I slowed my pace, wanting them to pass by. But they didn't. Instead, a voice said, "Adam."

I stopped and turned.

I think I said something like, "Sorry, you must be mistaken," because I heard a mumbled apology as someone brushed past me and headed off into the night. What I also remember is the small lapel pin he wore on his coat with the image of a colourful, twisting double helix. I don't know why I should remember this tiny detail, but I was positive I had seen that design somewhere before, and I *knew* it was significant.

The encounter must have unnerved me, because I gave up any idea of breaking and entering, and headed home, almost laughing at my own paranoia.

Almost.

That night I dreamed of colourful double-helix shapes; I dreamed of Arcadia.

I awoke, agitated and bewildered, wondering why it felt like I'd had this dream many times before.

My phone trilled impatiently, and my day began.

I came home early on Thursday afternoon, ready to go and collect Julia from school for her big competition – and that was when my world tilted frantically on its axis.

When I opened the door, Rachel came out of the kitchen, her hands covered in flour which she was absentmindedly wiping with a tea towel. She smiled. I smiled back, but my smile died the moment she spoke.

"Did you find your keys, love?"

I didn't say anything, but my expression must have said, 'What are you talking about?'

"Your *keys*," Rachel prompted. "You came home at lunchtime to get the spares; said you'd misplaced yours at work. You took the whole bunch."

My life shimmered as unreality rushed to envelop me.

Rachel was beginning to look worried, so I forced myself to smile reassuringly, producing my own keys. "Yeah," I said, hoping I sounded normal. "I got them. "

Rachel came over and kissed me gently, but her eyes seemed to be asking if I was okay.

I held on to her a little longer than necessary.

"I'm fine," I said, more for my own benefit than hers.

Rachel almost laughed. "What?" she asked. "I never said…"

"I know. I'm okay."

But I no longer believed this. In fact, I knew that I was far from okay.

I left, thinking only of her kiss, the feel of her body as I held her close.

I never wanted to forget how she felt, because I had a terrible feeling that it would be the last time I would ever see her.

The mental blackouts were becoming more frequent, my unreliable mind no longer able to fill in the blanks.

I'd heard something on the radio as I drove that caused me to brake suddenly and pull over, shaking and terrified, but by the time I arrived to pick up Julia, the feeling had gone.

I would recall everything much later, of course, as I stood in the rain looking into the face of the stranger who held the answers to the truth that would shatter my world. But before that, I had to collect my daughter from school.

•

I almost missed the look of surprise on her teacher's face when she saw me walking through the schoolyard, but now it's all I can see.

I don't remember what I said before I started shouting, but I do remember Miss Milner's face turning deathly white, her mouth opening and closing soundlessly and her wild-eyed look of panic.

"What do you mean Julia's gone?" I screamed, louder than I intended, more to compensate for my own sense of unreality and confusion, oblivious to the heads that turned in our direction as the conversations between other parents were put on hold.

Miss Milner's hand was now clutching at her throat. "I…" she stammered, her words stumbling over each other in desperation, "you… I mean… Mr Cross, you picked Julia up early. You said that…"

I had stopped listening to her by then. I remember my chest tightening enough to hurt, sending sharp, stabbing knives of pain through my body; blood pounded in my head, loud enough to drown out any other sounds as I turned and ran for the gates.

I have no memory of my panicked, undignified exit, but I do remember how I felt as I stood outside the school gates, staring at the place where my car should have been.

Rachel and Julia are my reason for living. I would never do anything to harm them.

But what if I have?

I have to phone Rachel, but I'm too scared.

What if she doesn't answer?

What if she does?

I wandered aimlessly around town for hours, trying to work up the courage to call Rachel. Grey clouds had begun to gather ominously, darkening the day and bringing with them the threat of a storm – perfectly matching my mood.

I had thrown away my mobile. I no longer believed it was secure; sometime between leaving Julia's school and the arrival of the thunder clouds, I had begun to worry that it could be used to track my movements.

As I approached the public phone at the end of the street, the first fat drops of rain began to fall. I reached for the handset, and, for some unexplained reason, I expected it to ring.

It didn't.

As I dialled home, I no longer felt anxious or afraid. All I felt was numb, empty, unreal.

For an awful moment, I was certain that the voice on the other end would not be Rachel's.

"Hello?" Of course, it was.

I exhaled.

"Rachel, it's me, Harry." I had no idea at all what to say or how to say it. All I could manage was, "Julia…"

The extended silence before Rachel answered stretched into eternity.

And her words, when she did speak, shattered my reality.

"Julia is here with me. And so is Harry. Who is this?"

She may have said more, but I had already hung up.

The payphone began to ring.

I knocked it out of the cradle, leaving it swinging.

I started to turn, sensing the presence of someone else only a fraction of a second before they spoke.

A single word. "Adam."

The man moved closer, blocking any chance of escape.

Rain poured from his black umbrella like a river, blurring his features, though I knew I had seen him before.

I recognised his lapel pin, the colourful double helix glimmering in the rain.

"What do you want?" I asked, not even bothering to protest that I was not Adam that I was, I *am… was…* Harry Cross.

The man smiled benignly. "There has been an unexpected development," was all he said.

And that was when I remembered what I'd heard on the radio earlier:

"A report received today from an undisclosed source suggests yet more controversy at CRL, the Cryogenic Research Laboratories, which came under investigation three years ago amongst allegations of illegal research into reproductive cloning: the cloning of an entire human being. Those allegations were never proven, and the facility went on to receive commendations for its work in the study of the effects of low temperatures on organisms for the purpose of achieving cryopreservation. But now, if these new allegations — that the research allegedly begun three years ago has actually been brought to fruition — are proven, there will undoubtedly be severe repercussions for the facility. We tried to speak to the head of the biotechnology department, but senior researcher Harry Cross was unavailable for comment."

"What's happening to me?" My whole body felt numb and I struggled to form the words. "Who… who am I?"

"Arcadia has attracted unwanted media attention." The

stranger replied by way of an answer. "They don't care about the significant progress we have made in the use of molecular nanotechnology, they only want the sensational; it's what sells. Human cloning is a minefield, even though you, my friend, should be worthy of a Pulitzer. It's going to be a rough ride, but CRL will weather the storm. We always do. There will be questions, but the biotechnology department will continue its official line of authorised research into somatic-cell nuclear transfer. Of course, Harry had to return to his family, and that means you need to come home."

He turned and walked away.

I followed him into the night, only vaguely aware of the faint buzz of the dialling tone coming from the slowly swaying receiver above the pounding of the rain.

Previously employed as an armed police officer in the MOD, then as a live music/karaoke entertainer in Spain, Tony Harrison now works as a full-time admin assistant and part-time writer, reading and writing horror, sci-fi and fantasy.

During the 90s he had several Gothic horror stories and some depressing poems published in a Goth fanzine called Pink Flamingo (no, he doesn't know, either!). More recently, the ghost stories 'Daddy's home' and '42' have appeared in the anthologies, In The Dark and Inkerman Street; the epic comedy poem 'Legend of Sam Sasquatch' in Picture This, and in 2018, the ghost story 'Resurrection Act' appeared in the Crossing The Tees anthology.

He is spending the 2020 lockdown working on a fantasy/ steampunk novel with his twelve-year-old nephew.

THE FAÇADE

MELISSA ROSE ROGERS

Frustrated, almost to tears – that was my status, but I couldn't post it. The night before had been long and thankless – the only reason I was still upright was the coffee carafe before me.

I deleted the post I had started writing. They wouldn't understand. My friends don't have kids, and when Tanissa said her puppy whining at night was comparable to my baby boy crying with colic for four hours straight, I just gritted my teeth and nodded. Scrolling through social media, all the posts were perfectly plated meals, colour coordinated bookcases, and complicated nail art – guilt inducing reminders of my disorganisation, microwave meals, and the dirt under my nails.

The baby monitor light blipped. I didn't hear anything, so it must have been Elijah rolling over and the microphone picked it up.

I kept scrolling. There was a recipe for overnight oats that looked good. I started reading it when I noticed the green line on the baby monitor again. I slid the volume up higher, and flipped on the display. Its monochrome colours revealed Elijah had turned to his side, his sleep sack billowing about him and the white rungs of the crib like a forest of birch trees.

I placed the monitor on the coffee table, and pulled my knees closer. Suffocated. Alone. That's how I felt. When I mentioned it to my mom, she dismissed me and said that in a few years I'd look back and think these were the happiest, most precious times of my life. Pretty discouraging. Just thinking about it made me feel like the rhythm I once knew, the freedoms I once had, were gone. I'd been condemned to an on-call 24/7 job where I'd never get to be myself again. Motherhood rebirthed me into someone I couldn't recognise. The bright green line on the display lit up again. I glanced up, and that's when I noticed it, the second hand. Just as tiny and precious as the outspread hand curled in slumbering contentment. I pressed the display button switching it off and on again. The hand was still there. What the hell? My heart leapt into my throat, and before I could think about it, I'd thrown myself up the beige carpeted stairs of our townhouse and flung open the hollow core door to the bedroom. The blinds were shut, the curtains drawn, and peaceful dim blanketed the room. Overhead, the ceiling fan spun its unchanging rhythm. I stalked to the crib, white against the eggshell white walls. I peeked over the crib, past the camera perched on the rail aimed to the right side of the crib where Elijah preferred.

There were two Elijahs. Identical in every way. Nausea washed over me. I'd heard of women having psychotic breaks after delivering babies, but I never thought it'd happen to me. I touched one hand – warm, soft skin. Tiny fingernails freshly trimmed. I touched the other hand on the other baby, expecting it to be an illusion, to push through the image to the minky blue crib sheet below. Instead, I felt soft warmth just like on the first baby. My breath rasped sharply – enough to wake the two babies.

Straight dark hair? Check. Laughing brown eyes? Check. Chubby-wubby cheeks? Check. They were just alike in every perceptible way. The baby on the left cooed. My baby's voice. The baby on the right cooed in just the same way.

"Elijah?" I said, my voice and hands quaking, bile rising in my throat.

Both sets of dark eyes focused on me, both smiles identical. My head spinning, I gripped the white railing but it didn't steady my insides. *This can't be happening. What exactly is happening?*

One of the babies reached toward me – but which one was real? They both cooed and gurgled – the typical baby noises that I'm used to. *Am I just going crazy? I mean, how could I forget I had twins? One of them is fake – but not a hallucination. What then?* I took a step backwards, I turned around and surveyed my bedroom – trying to centre myself in the familiar, the known. I focused on the *Live, Love, Laugh* canvas over the plain four-poster bed. The quilt was one of those bed-in-a-bag eight piece sets from JC Penney's – simple and dark blue. On the tall dresser, my picture and Darren's from that trip to Cancun sat in a place of honour next to my dark wood jewellery box. I turned back around, feeling just as off my rocker as before. Two identical baby boys were still watching me, eyes twinkling.

"Elijah," I said again, eyes darting from one to the other. They both gurgled and smiled.

One lifted his wiggly legs and rocked them back and forth. The one on the right did the same, then grabbed his feet, swaying to an unheard melody.

I booped one's nose, and then the other. They both giggled and looked at each other. Panic was surging through me. I wished he had a birthmark, a blemish of some sort, cradle cap, anything I could use to pick out which one was which.

"Say dada." I found myself forming the words with an expressionless face but I couldn't fake a sing-songy tone.

The baby on the left said, "Da... da." The second baby only gurgled.

"You," I pointed at the left one. "You're the fake. You're not real."

The tiny figure laughed at me, mischievous eyes glinting as it rolled to its side – something the real Elijah hadn't figured out how to do. "How did you know?" Its squeaky voice unnerved me.

"The real Elijah can't say 'dada' yet. The real Elijah can't roll over." My voice cracked.

"Good. I'll keep that in mind for next time." It cackled, standing in its footed pyjamas and teetering across the crib. The fake baby lurched itself over the rail, then dashed across my beige carpet. Instinct kicked in, and I chased after it.

"Next time?" I shouted, the fear in my voice multiplied. "What are you?"

"A fairy, stupid," it called as it scurried toward the front door.

Before I could register, the door burst open, letting in the afternoon glow. I stopped myself, and suburban noises filtered back to me, the grounding I had needed, a weed whacker in the distance, dogs yipping, a car horn on the nearby road. I sat numbly on the stairs and pulled my arms about me, as if my meagre warmth would quiet the shock I felt. Then a chirp carried down the stairs – my baby boy was trying out his voice. The real Elijah. I shut the front door and slid the deadbolt in place, knowing that would not be enough to make me feel safe again. *What would I have done if I had caught that thing?* My footsteps fell slow, mechanical up the stairs. In the bedroom, I stared at my perfect little baby for some time, before plucking him to my chest. He snuggled his head against my neck, not knowing why my heartbeat was ragged. I sank to the floor and rocked him back and forth, but it was more to comfort me. A tear slid down my face, but it wasn't frustration that brought me to it… it was this weird situation. *If I tell anyone, they'll think I'm crazy. Maybe if they think I'm crazy, they'll take my baby.* Loneliness and fear washed over me. *I can't tell anyone. Darren's already worried about me.* Downstairs, my phone started ringing – it was Darren's ringtone. I slowly stood, clutching the chattering baby against me and made my way back toward my anchor in the grown up world.

"Hey, hun," my husband's voice came through. "I think the camera's glitching. It was weird. When I pulled up the baby monitor app to check in on him, it looked like Elijah had an extra hand on the corner of the display. Maybe it's overheating and duplicating part of the display. Could you reset the camera?"

This was my chance. If I was going to tell him what I saw, it had better be right then, but I couldn't make the words come out.

"Hun? Can you hear me?"

"Yeah," I said, though my mind was racing along a dangerous precipice.

The fairy was real. I'm not crazy. How can I stop the fairy from coming back? I can't. I'm powerless. I'm trapped in this beige townhouse, a silencing prison. I'm trapped in this image of being a perfect mother – who selflessly cleans and cooks and wears pearls while vacuuming like Leave it to Beaver.

"Hun?" he asked again, that edge of worry creeping back in. "Is everything okay?"

"Yeah," I said, forcing the words into a calm, "I'll reset the camera."

Postpartum psychosis is a better answer, an answer with a solution – that's what I'm going to go with. A hallucination of a sleep-addled mind – none of this was real. Maybe if I swept this whole afternoon under my mental rug, wiped it off my mental slate and started over like a server reboot, like the camera I was supposed to reset, I could at least assume the façade of sanity. Maybe.

Melissa Rose Rogers draws inspiration from nature and is surrounded by a temperate rainforest with diverse species — the Great Smoky Mountains of Western North Carolina in the US where she, her husband, daughter, and furbabies live.

When she's not writing, you'll find her playing board games or experimenting in the kitchen. She loves reading, and especially enjoys Patricia C. Wrede, Tad Williams, and Peter V. Brett.

She usually follows people back on Twitter where she posts ridiculous memes and retweets excessively using the handle of @ MRogersWrites

Find our more at https://melissaroserogers.com/

THE SEVENTH ATTEMPT

R. BRUCE CONNELLY

Once upon a time, on the upper West Side of Manhattan, there was a little book store.

In the basement of the book store was a bathroom.

And in the bathroom, there was a little spider.

The clerks who worked in the book store didn't spend much time in his room. When they did come in, he would hide.

And if he didn't hide fast enough, some of them would make a great deal of noise when they saw him.

But there was one clerk who would read a newspaper in there on Sundays. He was a quiet sort, so the spider would creep out on his web to get a better look.

One Sunday, as the clerk sat reading and the spider sat peeking, a fly flew into the room. It flew right through the web and landed on the newspaper.

SWAT!

The clerk was about to flush the fly when he saw the spider.

"Here you go, " he said, and dropped the fly into the web.

"Thank you," said the spider.

"You're welcome," said the clerk.

The spider made a neat little bundle of the fly and tied it up in the web for supper. "What are you reading?" asked the spider.

"The New York Times," said the clerk. "It's the Arts and Leisure section."

"Oh," said the spider.

"I like to keep up with what's going on in the theatre," said the clerk.

"Oh," said the spider. "What is a 'theatre'?"

"They're wonderful places," said the clerk. "They're places where they put on plays. Hundreds of people go to watch them. There are actors who pretend to be the characters in those plays. They could be kings or pirates or..." He stopped. The little spider had raised one leg.

"Question?" asked the clerk.

"Yes," said the spider. "What are 'plays'?"

"Oh, gosh," said the clerk. "How can I explain plays? Have you ever been outside the bathroom?"

"I've been in the big room beyond, where all the books are kept."

"Okay," said the clerk. "Did you ever walk through any of the books?"

The spider nodded.

"Right. What books did you walk through?"

"There was one about some children who get half of what they wished for. And one where a family of dolls explore a floating island. And one about a flying boy..."

197

"Well, you could go to a theatre right now and see that boy fly! The whole story is being done right now in a big theatre on Broadway, only the boy is being played by a girl."

"How come?"

"He's got to sing pretty high," said the clerk, and sighed.

"Why do you sigh?" asked the spider, crawling a little further up the wall.

"Because that's what I want to be doing."

"Singing high?"

"Acting. This isn't my real job. I work here to pay the rent, but what I really want to be is an actor."

"What's an 'actor'?"

"ACK!" croaked the clerk, clutching at his throat and falling sideways against the wall.

"Are you alright?" cried the spider, running forward on his web.

"Fine," said the clerk, sitting back up again. "I was acting."

"That was acting?" asked the spider.

"You sound like my drama teacher," said the clerk. "Here, I'll show you." He closed the paper and pointed to the front page. "See? Those are actors. They are all drawn by Al Hirschfeld. These are the people who pretend to be the characters in the play."

"And you want to be one of them?"

"Mm hm."

"Why don't you?"

"There aren't a lot of plays casting right now. And you have to be really good to get in one of the plays that are." He folded the paper in half. "Look, you want to see something neat? The artist hides his daughter's name in the pictures. Her name is 'Nina'. He puts the number of how many times in the corner here. There are five 'Nina's in this one. See? There's one. And there? And here's one in the dress, see? And this one on the sleeve, sort of drawn way out? I can't find the fifth one."

The spider climbed to the ceiling and then dropped down on a web above the paper where he could see the whole picture better. He and the clerk studied the drawing together.

"There! There it is," cried the spider, pointing with four of his legs. "It's her hair! See?"

"Good for you!" laughed the clerk.

"Bruce!" a voice called from upstairs. "Bring some more 'Pat the Bunny' up, will you?"

"Gotta go," said the clerk. "I'll see you later."

"Is that your name?" asked the spider.

"Uh huh. Robert Bruce. What's yours?"

"I don't have one," said the spider. "I've never had anyone give me one. Most of those I meet are lunches."

"Well, I'll give you one," said the clerk. " I'll think up a really good one." He pulled the chain to turn off the light and closed the door. The spider crawled back down to his web and began his supper. "Robert Bruce," he mused. "Didn't I crawl over a story about him once?"

Some time later, the door opened, the light came on and in came the clerk.

"Renfield," he called.

The spider peeked out. 'Who?" he asked.

"Renfield!" said Bruce. " That's your name."

"It is?"

"Sure. I brought a fly for you. It was buzzing around the front desk and I got it with a swatter."

"Thank you," said the spider. "That's very nice. Why is my name Renfield?"

"Did you ever crawl over 'Dracula'?" asked Bruce.

"No," said the spider.

"There's this character in the book who eats flies and says, 'Blood is the Life '."

"And so it is, " said the spider.

"There you are!" said, Bruce. "I named you after him!"

"Thank you," said the spider.

After that, the clerk and the spider became great friends. Bruce would bring the papers in on Sunday so they could find the 'Nina's together, and he brought every fly he swatted to the spider. Renfield enjoyed the company and he was happy not to have to worry about where his next meal was coming from. They talked at length about theatre, and one day, as they were poring over the trade papers, Renfield spotted an advertisement.

"Look!" he said. "They need someone to play me!"

There, beneath the spider, was an ad calling for actors to audition for a company of 'Dracula' to be performed on Broadway.

"That's the character I told you about," said Robert

Bruce. "He's the one who eats flies. But I'm afraid you're a little short for it. He has to be 5'6"."

Renfield eyed the clerk with a practiced eye. "Aren't you 5'6"?"

"Yes," said the clerk. "But… these things are always cast in advance. They only put the auditions in the paper because the union makes them."

"Maybe," said the spider. "It couldn't hurt to go see, could it?"

"It'd be a waste of time," said the clerk. "Besides, I have a lot of books to stock upstairs."

"Seems to me," said Renfield, "the only thing keeping you from being an actor is you, yourself."

"Hm," said the clerk.

"Go after it!"

"Well…"

"Go on," said the spider, giving him a little push.

"But I've gone to lots of these and nothing's happened."

"So go to another," said Renfield. "Go on! What would happen if I stopped hunting flies after missing the first six?"

Bruce smiled. "You're right," he said. "I'll ask for the afternoon off."

"That's the boy," said the spider, patting him on the back with three of his legs.

The clerk got up and left the bathroom. He came back a second later. "Oh, Renfield?" he called. "Here's your lunch!" And he tossed him a fly.

"I got an audition, Renfield!"

The spider almost fell out of his web as Bruce blew in like a gust of wind.

"I go back tomorrow!"

The spider clapped his legs together. "That's great! See what I told you?"

"I'd hug you," said the clerk, " but that would skoosh you. So take this nice big fly as a thank you." He tossed the fly into the web.

"Watch this," said Renfield. "This is how a spider goes to get his food. You may be able to use this tomorrow."

Bruce watched carefully as Renfield scuttled quickly forward a few inches on his web and then gingerly, leg by leg, crept up toward the fly until he was almost upon it…

…then he pounced!

"Great," said the clerk. "I'll use it!"

He got the part.

He and the spider were very happy. Thanks to the attention of the clerk, Renfield was now the size of a dime, so well had he been fed. The two of them celebrated in the basement of the bookstore.

"And you cinched it for me," Bruce told him. "For part of my audition, I had to pretend to catch a fly. I did just what you showed me and they said they had never seen anything so creepy!"

" 'Creepy'?" asked Renfield.

"Creepy for them. Natural for you."

"Oh. What happens now?"

"We go into rehearsal now for three weeks in Philadelphia. Then we'll play a week there before bringing the play into the City."

"So, I won't see you for awhile," said Renfield.

"No, but I'll be back as soon as we get to New York."

"I know it," said Renfield, trying to smile. "Will you... will you be working here at the bookstore?"

"No, now I'll be working in a theatre like I showed you in the New York Times."

"Will Mr Hirschfeld draw a picture of you on the front page of the Arts and Leisure section?"

"Wouldn't that be great?"

"Mm hm," said Renfield. "Then I could... see you."

"Yeah! And try to find the 'Nina's in my costume!"

"Yup."

"It's all due to you, you know, Renfield. And I'll bring the cast back to meet you as soon as we get into town."

"What's a 'cast'?"

"A group of actors. All the people in the show."

"Okay," said the spider.

"And I'll make sure the other clerks here bring you flies every day."

But they didn't.

One was too scared. She didn't even use the bathroom since Bruce had discovered Renfield in the corner. She'd waited until she got home.

Another clerk hit the flies alright, but never saw where they landed.

A third forgot completely about him, so tied up was she in running the bookstore.

Renfield had gotten so used to having his flies brought to him that he'd neglected his web. Any flies that came through were able to escape easily. Once, when the door opened and the light came on he ran out to greet the lady; she saw him coming for her at a great speed, screamed and slammed the door. No flies came in through a closed door. Sometimes no one came into the room for days. As time passed with no food, he got smaller and smaller. He set about making a new web, but it was more difficult as he lost strength. He was able to catch a couple of small roaches in it. That helped, but one day a water beetle fell through it and broke it up, leaving Renfield with tatters.

On a Sunday three weeks later, one of the clerks left the Arts and Leisure section in the bathroom. Renfield crawled over to it and there, on the front page, was a Hirschfeld drawing of 'Dracula', due to open in New York in one more week. There was Dracula, and Mina and Jonathan Harker, and yes, his friend, his namesake, wearing funny pyjamas with seven 'Nina's hidden in the pattern.

Renfield was so happy for his friend.

And so lonely.

And very hungry.

He could barely make it back up the wall to his web. He crouched in the entrance hole waiting for someone to bring him a fly.

But no one did.

The door opened. The room filled with light.

"Renfield!"

The spider opened five of his eyes. Was that...? It was! Robert Bruce was back! How long had he slept? He felt so small and so hungry.

"This is Renfield, everybody," said Bruce.

"We hear you inspired our Renfield," said a tall dark man in a deep voice. "Thank you."

Renfield slowly lifted one leg in greeting, but it fell back to his side.

"What happened?" Bruce asked the spider, kneeling down beside him. Renfield didn't answer. Bruce pulled a piece of tissue from his pocket and unwrapped two flies which he placed beside the spider.

"These are from my dressing room," he said. "There are lots of flies there. Could you eat a little something?"

"Thank you," murmured Renfield, and weakly began his lunch.

"Excuse me, everybody," Bruce said. "Could I speak to him alone? He doesn't look well."

"Of course," said a lovely lady, with platinum hair and a white fur piece. "Exquisite meeting you, Renfield, dear."

"See you around, chum," called a robust fellow with lots of curly hair.

When the cast had left, Bruce turned to the spider. "Renfield?"

The spider slowly looked up at his friend.

"Haven't you been eating?" he asked, gently.

"No," said the spider.

"Why not?" Bruce demanded.

"I don't know," said Renfield, starting in on the second fly. "I… guess they forgot about me."

"So why didn't you feed yourself?"

"Hm?"

"Why didn't you look after yourself?"

"Oh… I…"

"You were feeding yourself long before I came along. Didn't you tell me that if I didn't take care of myself that no one else would?"

"Yes," said the spider, smiling a bit. "I guess I got used to my meals being delivered."

"And that's my fault," said Bruce. "But, look. I have an idea. Since you can't take care of yourself…"

"I can, too," said Renfield, bristling.

"Okay, why don't you come prove it? My dressing room has lots of flies. You can come with me and move in there."

"Into a theatre?" asked the spider.

"Yep. Of course, you'll have to build a new web."

"I can do that," Renfield said.

Bruce offered his arm and Renfield slowly climbed up it.

"Be careful. Find a spot where I won't skoosh you."

Renfield settled up by the collar of Bruce's coat.

"Did you know," said the actor, "no one named Robert Bruce can skoosh a spider?"

"Why?"

"It has to do with Robert the Bruce, the Scottish King who learned from a spider to keep trying. He was hiding from his enemies in a barn and he watched a spider trying to build a web over and over but the wind kept breaking the strand. On the seventh attempt, the spider succeeded and the King realised if a spider can do it, so can he, and he went out and defeated his enemies."

"I bet that was the story I crawled over one night."

"I bet it was," laughed Bruce, climbing the stairs. "How do you like my friends?"

"They look just like Hirschfelds," said Renfield, "only without the Ninas."

Bruce settled the spider into the dressing room on the third floor of the theatre and got ready for the performance. If he left the door open, Renfield could see the stage three floors below.

It was perfect.

After his first scene, Bruce returned to the dressing room, excited to ask the spider what he'd thought.

But Renfield didn't look well at all. He was huddled up in one corner of his new web.

As Bruce slowly approached, Renfield looked up weakly and fell out of his web. A thin strand of silk spun out behind him, stopping him before he hit the floor. He gave a shuddering breath... and hung limp.

"Renfield! No!" cried Bruce, kneeling quickly. "Are you alright?"

The spider hung there, still.

Then he opened one eye.

"Acting," whispered the spider and winked.

•

R. Bruce Connelly is a professional actor, director and Muppet who lives in New York City. He has had four stories in his 'Bike Cycle' series published in

Harvey Duckman Presents… Volumes 1-4, plus a short story in Harvey's Christmas Special 2019.

This story takes place in a bookstore that no longer exists but was the inspiration for the movie, You've Got Mail. The bathroom referred to did exist and was basically a water closet in which the Creature from the Black Lagoon would have felt at home.

The spider lived there as well.

Also available from Sixth Element Publishing
in paperback and eBook:

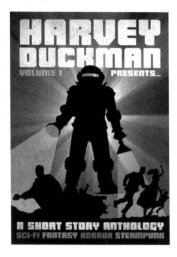

Harvey Duckman Presents… Volume 1
Published April 2019
*including stories by: Kate Baucherel,
D.W. Blair, A.L. Buxton, R. Bruce Connelly,
Nate Connor, Marios Eracleous,
Craig Hallam, C.G. Hatton, Mark Hayes,
Peter James Martin, Reino Tarihmen, J.L. Walton,
Graeme Wilkinson and Amy Wilson.*

www.6epublishing.net

Also available from Sixth Element Publishing
in paperback and eBook:

Harvey Duckman Presents... Volume 2

Published July 2019

*including stories by: Phil Busby, A.L. Buxton,
J.S. Collyer, R. Bruce Connelly, Phoebe Darqueling,
Lynne Lumsden Green, Craig Hallam, Jon Hartless,
Mark Hayes, Andy Hill, Fred Johnson, Peter James Martin,
Ben McQueeney and A.D. Watts.*

www.6epublishing.net

Also available from Sixth Element Publishing
in paperback and eBook:

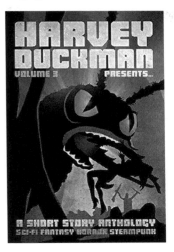

Harvey Duckman Presents... Volume 3
Published October 2019
*including stories by: Peter James Martin, Ben McQueeney,
A.L. Buxton, R. Bruce Connelly, Phoebe Darqueling,
Melissa Wuidart Phillips, Marios Eracleous, Nate
Connor, James Porter, Joseph Carrabis, Cheryllynn Dyess,
Erudessa Gentian, Liz Tuckwell, JL Walton and Amy Wilson,
as well as a bonus 'Harvey Duckman' story by Mark Hayes,
and a foreword by Craig Hallam.*

www.6epublishing.net

Also available from Sixth Element Publishing
in paperback and eBook:

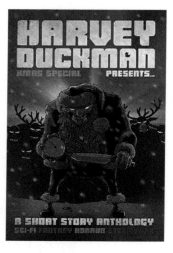

Harvey Duckman Presents…
Christmas Special 2019
Published December 2019
including stories by: Thomas Gregory, Andy Hill,
Peter James Martin, Craig Hallam, Kate Baucherel,
Cheryllynn Dyess, Marios Eracleous, Zack Brooks,
Ben McQueeney, Maggie Kraus, Gerald Wiley,
Lynne Lumsden Green, Mark Hayes,
Ben Sawyer and R. Bruce Connelly.

www.6epublishing.net

Also available from Sixth Element Publishing
in paperback and eBook:

Harvey Duckman Presents... Volume 4
Published March 2020
including stories by: Adrian Bagley, Crysta K Coburn,
Thomas Gregory, Christine King, Peter James Martin,
John Holmes-Carrington, A.L. Buxton, Zack Brooks,
Fred Johnson, Ben McQueeney, Keld Hope, Deborah
Barwick, Jon Hartless, R. Bruce Connelly, and Mark Hayes,
as well as a bonus 'Harvey Duckman' story by Andy Hill,
and a foreword by Amy Wilson.

www.6epublishing.net

Find Harvey on Facebook:
www.facebook.com/harveyduckman

Find Harvey on Twitter:
twitter.com/DuckmanHarvey

•

Sixth Element Publishing
www.6epublishing.net

•

About C.G. Hatton

CG Hatton is the author of the fast-paced, military science fiction books set in the high-tech Thieves' Guild universe of galactic war, knife-edge intrigue, alien invasion, thieves, assassins, bounty hunters and pirates. She also edits and writes in the Harvey Duckman Presents... series of scifi, fantasy, steampunk and horror short story anthologies. The first book in the main Thieves' Guild series, Residual Belligerence, is free to download for Kindle.

Printed in Poland
by Amazon Fulfillment
Poland Sp. z o.o., Wrocław

61878027R00132